The Tower Of Emrys

By Ian Wilson

Ian Wilson

2022

First Printing: 2022

ISBN: 978-1-7351243-9-1
Ian T. Wilson 46 Edward st.Malone, New York, 12953
https://legendsandsongs.weebly.com

To Tom, Amy, Sarah, and Lisa

Pronunciation guide

Taliesin: tale-YES-in

Gwion: g-WEE-on

Gwyn: g-WIN

Creirwy: CREER-wee

Emrys Wledig: EM-ris LED-dig

Uther: OO-thur

Ceridwen: CARE-id-when

Tegid- TEG-id

Nimue: NIM-weh

Kynyr: kin-NOOR

Annwyn: AN-new-win

Igerna: ee-GURN-ah

Gorlois: gor-LO-is

Prologue

My nostrils tingled with the scent of roast boar, venison, poultry, pickled vegetables, bread and cakes. It was Christmas Day and King Emrys had hosted a lavish feast for his nobles and knights in the great hall of Camelot. As High King, he sat at the head of the table. At his right sat the queen, Nimue, and at his left sat his brother, Lord Uther.

All eyes and ears were fixed on me, the Chief Bard of Britain, as my fingers ran over the lyre strings, plucking chords and melodies. Songs of the great kings and warriors of old flowed out from my throat like a river of music.

As the last song ended, King Emrys raised his cup in a toast.

"To Taliesin, the prince of bards!"

"Hear, hear!" said King Kynyr of Dyfed.

With humble acceptance, I bent my head in thanks for their sincere praise.

"And to the brave men of Britain," I added, "who give us reason to sing."

We drained our cups.

"We've heard strangely little of the acts of King Emrys," said Kynyr, wiping the mead from his red beard.

"That is because the acts of Emrys are well known here," replied Emrys modestly.

"Not to us," said the young Morgana, daughter of Gorlois of Cornwall.

"Aye, ye were not yet born when his majesty defeated the tyrant Vortigern," said Kynyr.

"That is a story I have not yet heard," I remarked.

The high king chuckled. "It is a long tale."

"I like long tales," said Morgana eagerly.

"There are yet many days of Christmastide," observed Lord Gorlois. "Surely you may give a full accounting in that time."

"I would very much like to hear it from your own lips, good king," I added. "For the records."

"Fine, fine!" relented Emrys. "I shall indulge you."

The king sat back, took another sip of beer, and began the tale that I shall here relate.

1

    I was only sixteen summers old when it happened; barely more than a boy, and ill-equipped for all that had befallen me. My wrists chafed from the ropes binding me to the mast of the Saxon longboat as it rocked to and fro on the frothing sea. My stomach twisted in knots, partly from the rolling of the sea, partly from what had occurred hours earlier. I had been trained in the arts of war from a very young age, but nothing prepared me for the experience of actually killing a man for the first time. I could not shake the feeling of guilt at taking another's life. I understood why some men avoided violence altogether rather than endure it.

The Saxon men at the oars grunted, straining toward the setting sun. At least I thought they were Saxon. I had never seen a Saxon before that day, but they seemed to fit my Uncle Aldrien's description of them: tall and muscular with long, fair hair and beards. I wondered how long it had been since the last time they bathed.

One of the Saxons, who appeared to be their chieftain, approached me, thrusting a skin of water in my face

"Drink!" he barked in my native Cumbric language, his Saxon accent as heavy as iron.

I did as I was ordered. The Saxon smirked and muttered something in his native tongue.

Night fell as land came into view: the fair green isle of Britain, the land of my birth. I had not seen that country since my mother took us to live at my Uncle's manor in Armorica. Ten summers had come and gone since then.

Up the Thames into Londinium we sailed. Once they had tied up the boat to the busy harbor, my captors unbound me from the mast and dragged me, squirming and struggling, into the city.

"Release me, you barbarian swine!" I shouted.

A dull pain shot through my skull as the barbarian's hand struck me. "Quiet, bastard!"

They took me to a great house in the midst of the city, where a host of armed men greeted us. In their company was one of the cruelest-looking men I had ever laid eyes on. His deeply set, yellow-brown eyes were constantly looking about, as if always aware of possible threats. A purple cloak hung over his tunic and breeches, designating him as nobility. All this pointed to one fact: this was none other than Vortigern himself.

I stared into his face like a lion stares at a deer it is about to kill, rage burning in my heart with the intensity of a smith's forge. This was the man who murdered my father, and would have murdered my brother and I, had he gotten the chance to do so. He was the one who returned the land to heathenry and brought the Saxon scourge upon us.

"Is this he?" asked Vortigern.

"Of course it's him!" replied the Saxon, gruffly. "Does his highness not trust his servant Hengist?

"I have learned to trust that the Saxons have no end of tricks."

A harsh laugh rose from the barbarian's throat. The usurper squinted his fox-like eyes at me.

"Are you Emrys?" asked Vortigern, sneering with contempt.

Drawing in a deep breath, I spat full in Vortigern's face. His boney hand struck my cheek; the taste of my own blood filled my mouth. The Saxons roared with laughter.

"Perhaps you do not know who is speaking to you, boy," he growled.

"I know exactly who is speaking to me," I replied through clenched teeth. "The pretender, Vortigern."

"Say whatever your heart fancies, bastard," spat Vortigern. "I will not be troubled with your insolence much longer."

At a single motion from Vortigern's hand, the attendants dragged me away to a small outbuilding behind the main house. A great oaken door with a small slit about head height guarded the threshold; I gathered that this was the dungeon. I heard the sound of a large bolt sliding within and the great door swung open. A dark-colored mastiff took in my scent as the guard dragged me to a cell and chained me to the wall.

The dungeon was dank; a single window to the far end provided the only fresh air. A putrid scent permeated the place, turning my empty stomach. I wondered why Vortigern had not killed me yet; so far as I could tell, I was of little value to him alive. Would I be executed like a common criminal? Was I to be a victim in a gruesome sacrifice? What would become of my mother and my brother?

Rather than waste my mental energies on these musings, I thought it better to focus on finding a means of escape. This, too, proved futile; my chains were stout, as were the iron bars on the door of the cell. Beyond that, I still had to contend with the dog, to say nothing of the guard. It seemed that I was doomed.

The approach of booted feet followed by a turn of a key in the lock interrupted my contemplation of my fate. Upon entering my cell, Hengist laid a bowl of stew at my feet and sat down on an overturned bucket. I looked at the bowl, then at the man who brought it. The thought that the stew could be poisoned had occurred to me, but why would Vortigern bother poisoning me when he could simply have me publicly executed?

"Well? Eat it!" he urged. "It isn't poisoned!"

The Saxon's assurances only raised my suspicions even further. I glared at his freckled face flickering in the candlelight, saying nothing.

"You aren't much for conversation, are you, lad?" said Hengist.

My jaw worked with pent-up anger at this foreign invader who dared treat me, a prince of Britain, in such a manner.

"Fine," said the barbarian, "if you're not going to eat, I will."

Taking the bowl from the floor, Hengist drank down the stew with great relish. My stomach rumbled loudly in protest; I had eaten nothing since early that morning, before the hunting trip that put me here in the first place.

"Who told you you could talk that way to the king?" the barbarian inquired, wiping drops of broth from his red-golden beard.

"He is no king," I grunted. "He killed my father and stole his throne."

"That's politics, I suppose," said Hengist. "Among my people, victory is all that matters. If you want to be the king, you have to kill the king. Bloody business. That's why I'm a mercenary, not a politician."

"What are you going to do with me?" I inquired.

"Take you into the mountain country."

"Why?"

"I don't rightly know, princeling," replied Hengist. "I'm just a sword for hire. I was told to go to Armorica, kidnap some spoiled bastard, and drag him back to Londinium. Soon as we get to the mountain country, I'll get paid, and you'll get what's coming to you."

"Why do you and Vortigern call me a bastard?" I growled. "My father was King Custennin!"

"That's what you think."

"What is that supposed to mean?"

Ignoring my query, the barbarian rose up and departed the dungeon. Impotent rage burned in my chest at the very thought that he might accuse my mother of infidelity. I would cut his heathen throat! How could he say that Custennin was not my father? What did he know? If Custennin was not my father, then who was?

Eventually, these and all other thoughts vanished in the realm of dreams. Like Taliesin, I am sometimes given visions of the future, though with lesser frequency.

A dreadful sight met my gaze that night: two wyrms, one red, the other white, locked in combat, writhing on the ground, snapping at each other with deadly teeth. I watched in horrified fascination, but as quickly as it had begun, it ended. I fell into a dreamless sleep.

2

I awoke with gasp as frigid water splashed on my face.

"Rise and shine!" said the coarse voice of Hengist as I lay gasping and sputtering on the floor.

After unlocking my chains, the barbarian's powerful, calloused hand grasped my arm, dragging me from the dungeon out into the courtyard. Now was my chance; with my free hand, I snatched Hengist's fighting knife from his belt, slicing his arm. The Saxon uttered what I can only assume was a curse, released me and backed away, drawing a short sword.

"I need him alive!" cried Vortigern from across the courtyard.

I looked about; Saxon mercenaries and British soldiers surrounded me, but none of them dared come near for fear of being sliced or stabbed; all but one, that is. A blunt object hit the back of my skull, and all was darkness after that.

I eventually awoke, my head throbbing. I found myself chained hand and foot to a cart, travelling westward through the snow-covered countryside. I need not bore you with the details of the long, dreary ride into the mountains. I said nothing to anyone the entire trip, save my prayers to the Almighty for deliverance.

We stopped at a tavern for the night; the last one before we went into those mysterious mountains. Vortigern had me placed in the stables with the horses. There was probably a guard not far away. It was comfortable enough, save for the smell of manure, a scent that I am not unaccustomed to. A small boy entered my stall with a bowl of pottage. His blue-grey eyes seemed filled with a combination of wonder and confusion as he placed the bowl on the floor.

"Thank you," I said.

"Is it true?" asked the boy.

"Is what true?"

"That you're the king?"

I paused, unsure how to answer, or even if I should answer.

"Yes, it is true."

I took the warm bowl in my chained hands and began to eat. It was peasant's fare, yes, but I have dined on worse. My mother always taught me to eat whatever was put in front of me and be thankful for it. After all, we are not guaranteed another meal. Furthermore, I was famished.

The stable boy stood there, watching, his face flickering in the warm light of an oil lamp.

"Is King Vortigern going to kill you?" he asked.

"Not if I can help it," I replied.

"How will you stop him?"

"I do not know that yet, but I am certain I will find a way."

"The old men in the village say that you are coming to restore the kingdom. Father says it is just a fable."

"I certainly hope your father is wrong."

"Me too," said the boy grimly. "I do not like King Vortigern, and I do not like his gods. They frighten me."

"They should," I replied.

Tears well up in the stable boy's eyes.

"They have eaten some of my friends. I fear one day they may eat me, too."

"Not if I have anything to say about it."

A voice from outside the stable called to the boy. Taking one last look at me, he ran out of the stall, shutting the stable door behind him, enclosing me in the dank, gloomy stable. After finishing my meal, I said my evening prayers, and fell asleep on a bed of straw.

The next morning, Hengist literally dragged me out of bed. Being fully conscious, I was compelled to walk, rather than ride in the cart. Hengist pulled me along by a chain like a dog. Cold, hunger and weariness were no strangers to me; this humiliation, however, was unbearable.

The western mountain country is a mysterious place, populated by trolls, dwarves, witches, and unnamed horrors. In the midst of it stood the cursed city of Bala, home of Tegid the god of sorcery, and his consort, Ceridwen, mistress of darkness.

Ever since I was a young lad, I had heard tales of those two. It is said that they had traversed the unplumbed depths between the spheres. Some say that Ceridwen had been fathered by Appolyon, the angel of the Pit. It is also said that they must drink the blood of youths to keep their magic strong, and to live forever. As a result of so many fantastical legends, I had almost thought them a work of fiction. Almost.

Their evil seemed to permeate the very stones. All were ill at ease. Even the Saxons had quieted their coarse conversation. Vortigern alone seemed undaunted by those brooding mountains. He worshipped evil; he had no discomfort when surrounded by its presence. The man turned my stomach.

In those haunted dales lay the remains of some ancient kingdom; great stones stood sentinel over the mountain passes, bearing witness to its former grandeur. Perhaps the unholy kingdom of Bala was the only remnant of a much larger kingdom of antiquity. I did not know with any certainty.

As we made camp under a canopy of rock, it seemed the night itself was alive. I could feel the gaze of something malevolent watching us. Perhaps Ceridwen herself had come. At any rate, I prayed for protection from whatever it was.

Vortigern and his men were seated about the campfire, while I sat a short distance away, huddled in my hunting cloak for warmth. My wrists chafed from the heavy chains holding me. Hengist came near, bearing a bowl of stew from the pot which he set before me.

"Perhaps you'll have the good sense to eat it this time," growled the barbarian. I glared back at him.

"Dirty looks will do you no good," he replied.

"They will do me no harm, either," I retorted.

The Saxon chuckled. "Still not giving up, you?"

"Not until I breathe my last breath."

"That may be sooner than you think, lad." With that, Hengist returned to the campfire.

I picked up the bowl, and gave thanks for it. If it was poisoned, then my death was the will of the Almighty. After finishing the meal, I lay down, attempting to get a little rest; sleep proved elusive, however, as I could still feel the hateful gaze of the Night watching me as I lay there, to say nothing of being half-frozen.

3

A silent snow fell upon the wilderness as morning crept over the cursed hills. We had continued on in our journey, walking through the snow-covered glens toward I knew not where.

About midday, an overwhelming sense of dread crept over me. It affected the horses as well; they knickered and whinnied, shifting back and forth. Slowly and steadily came the march of hundreds of iron-shod feet through the wilderness toward us. Out of that misty wilderness came an unspeakably gruesome army, led by a rider clothed in a long, black cloak. There was something odious about the rider that I could not name.

When Vortigern and his host knelt before him, I realized that this could be none other than Tegid himself. Despite my knocking knees, I was resolved to stand tall; I kneel for no god of heathenry.

A crooked grin split the false god's face when he looked at me. My blood chilled when I gazed into Tegid's eyes; it was like looking into the gates of Hell itself. Still, I did not look away.

"I see you have brought the sacrifice," said Tegid.

I swallowed hard. I came to the sickening realization that *I* was to be a sacrificial victim to satiate the god's bloodlust.

"Indeed, my lord," said Vortigern, still kneeling. "Forgive the impiety."

"Why do you not kneel, bastard?" asked the Lord of Bala.

"I do not kneel before heathen gods," I said defiantly.

"You will soon enough," Tegid answered threateningly as he turned his horse.

Accompanied by Tegid and his abominable host, we resumed our journey into the mountains. Presently, we came to a round-topped mountain where masons and other craftsmen labored, building some manner of fortification. As we neared this mountain fort, a young man approached us; he was the younger image of Vortigern, arrayed as a prince in a purple cloak with a gold torc about his neck. His hazel eyes briefly looked on me with an expression akin to pity.

"Greetings, Father," said the prince.

"Greetings, Vortimer," responded Vortigern. "It happened again, did it not?"

"Yes, Father," affirmed Prince Vortimer, looking at the earth.

"We will put an end to it on the new moon," said Tegid ominously.

The prince's countenance paled. "Is there no other way?" he inquired.

"No, there is not," replied the lord of Bala, eyeing me the way a cat looks at a mouse it is about to eat. "Take him to the stable."

Unlocking my chain from the cart, Hengist and Vortimer dragged me to a ramshackle structure not far from the hill that served as a stable for the horses and other beasts.

"Do I need a minder, now?" asked the Saxon, derisively.

"I am only ensuring my father's wishes are carried out," replied Vortimer.

"I've served your father well these past ten winters," the Saxon growled. "I don't need to be told how to do my duty by a whelp!"

Brushing Vortimer aside, the barbarian stalked away. Vortimer looked down at me with a melancholy expression.

"I am truly sorry for what my father is about to do," he said, apologetically, "but he is convinced that only your blood will placate the gods."

"When all is said and done," I replied in a voice just above a whisper, "your father will burn."

I did not know at the time where such a pronouncement proceeded from, but I knew it to be true. Somehow, I would survive this ordeal, and I knew that Vortigern would answer for his crimes.

Vortimer became even paler, if that was possible. Turning away, he left me there, chained to a post. My chains were loose enough that I could move my arms a little, and I could sit down and rise up if need be, but that was all.

Despite my premonition that I would escape this grisly fate, I had no notion as to how that would be done. I had no allies that I knew of and no means of escape that I could discern. One hope remained for me: that the Lord of life would provide a miraculous rescue.

I was afforded little comfort that night. I had my hunting cloak, and a roof over my head to keep the snow out, but that was all. Other men would have surrendered to despair by now, but I had been trained to accept whatever circumstances I found myself in. With that in mind, I spent much of my boyhood learning to withstand poor weather and other hardships. Still, it was a cold night; perhaps I would die of exposure before the new moon, robbing Vortigern of his prize. I chuckled softly, thinking of how my death would gall Vortigern.

Footsteps crunched through the newfallen snow outside the stable, drawing nearer to me. In the dark I could only barely make out the shape of a man. There was clattering noise, as of a bundle of sticks, and the sound of flint and steel. Soon a small fire lit up the night.

The firelight illuminated the pale face of Prince Vortimer, warming his hands in the flame. The meagre warmth felt good after hours of cold.

"Good evening, my lord," said the prince.

"Good evening," I replied sullenly. It seemed strange to me that the son of my greatest enemy should offer me such kindness. I was, indeed, suspicious of his motives, especially after I prophesied his father's death.

Vortimer placed a tripod above the flame and set a small cauldron upon it to cook whatever was inside.

"Trying to keep me fat for the slaughter?" I asked.

"Only seeking to offer a bit of kindness, my lord," replied the prince.

"What do you mean 'my lord'?" I asked.

"You have more right to the title than I do."

"That is not what your father says."

"What do you mean by that?"

"He is of the belief that King Custennin was not my real father."

Vortimer went silent for a moment, looking into the fire with a dour expression.

"According to Ceridwen, he was not."

"She lies," I growled.

"It does not matter," said Vortimer, continuing to stare at the flames. "You have acted with greater nobility than I have. I have been a coward, too afraid to defy my father to his face."

The horses and other beasts within the stable began stirring, nickering and whinnying with a strange nervousness. A sudden, violent quaking shook the stable, like the whole world was being ripped apart at the seams.

"Damn it, not again!" exclaimed Vortimer as he attempted to stabilize the cauldron.

I saw again the vision of the wyrms in combat and immediately I knew why the ground shook. Eventually, the quaking ceased, at least for a moment. Taking the lid from the cauldron, Vortimer ladled out some porridge into a bowl, and set it within reach of my chained arms. Gratefully, I raised the bowl to my lips and devoured the warm contents; it felt like the first meal I had eaten in months.

"The quakes are not Tegid's doing, you know," I said between mouthfuls of porridge.

Vortimer stared at me like I had grown a second head.

"How do you know that?"

"I know things," I replied.

"What is causing the quakes, then?"

"Conqueror Wyrms."

"And you know this with certainty?"

"Aye," I responded. "As certain as I am of anything."

Raising his hand to his jaw, Vortimer looked away toward the tower.

"Let us say that I believe you; even if I were to convince my father of the accuracy of your tale, he will probably go through with the sacrifice anyway."

"Then help me escape," I replied impatiently.

Vortimer said nothing after that. I did not then know whether his silence meant he would help me or not. Perhaps he was weighing his options. At any rate, I was grateful for his company in this dark hour.

4

The sun arose the next morning behind a curtain of grey cloud as I awoke from my slumbers. From without, I could hear faintly the sounds of men repairing the tower atop the hill.

Vortimer entered the structure, bearing a warm bowl of porridge.

"I imagine you have probably had enough of porridge by now," said the prince. "But this is the best I can do."

"Better than starvation," I replied, taking the bowl.

"Help is coming," said Vortimer, suddenly.

I looked up at the man, quizzically.

"You will be free soon," he clarified.

"When? How?"

Ignoring my questions, the prince turned away and left the stable. I did not know whether I trusted him yet or not. I was left with little choices, and if it proved to be some sort of trap, I was a condemned man anyway.

The dreary day passed into a frigid night. From the hilltop came abysmal druidic chanting. It was the new moon, after all, and my death was near at hand. If my rescue were coming, it would have to be soon.

Footsteps ever so slightly disturbed the snow nearby; had I not been trained as a hunter, I would not have heard them at all. Someone was approaching stealthily through the moonless night. The footsteps entered the stable. It occurred to me that this was one of the druids coming to take me to my doom, therefore I steeled myself for a fight to the death, either mine or his.

"Fear not, your highness," said a soft voice. I did not recognise who had spoken, but somehow I knew my rescue had come.

My shackles loosened and fell from my wrists and ankles. At last, I was free! A hand gasped my arm, leading me out of the stable and into the pitch-black wilderness away from that detestable hill. Like stalking wildcats, we crept carefully through the undergrowth.

Suddenly, a blood-curdling cry of rage and anguish erupted from the camp behind us; the druids had discovered my escape.

"Run!" said my guide.

My rescuer dragged me through the darkness. Twigs and brambles gasped at my cloak, but we stopped for nothing. The the baying of hounds followed us through the snowy wilds; soon they would be upon us.

My rescuer uttered a word in a language I did not understand. Seemingly in response, a howling wind from the north came up, filling in our tracks with snow and confusing the dogs.

Moments later, my rescuer dragged me into an even deeper darkness, which I thought to be a cave. There was a faint whisper in a language I did not understand, and within moments, a fire lit up the cavern. By the fire sat a young man in huntsman's garb, looking at me through sharp, blue-green eyes. He was roughly my own age, possibly a bit younger. Dark, short-cropped hair framed a pale, angular face. Pointed ears protruded from the sides of his head. *An elf, then*, I thought.

"Who are you?" I asked.

"I am Hefin," replied the young man, smiling.

"I am called Emrys," I returned.

"I know your name, sire," said Hefin. "We have been waiting for your return."

"'We'?"

"The elves of Avalon."

No one had seen the elves since my father's death, and they were a rare sight before then. They preferred to interfere with the affairs of ordinary men as little as possible, only appearing when it was absolutely necessary. The circumstances must truly be dire for one of their number to be here.

"You should rest now, my liege," said Hefin. "You have far to go in the morning and you will need your strength."

"What of the druids?" I asked.

"They cannot find us down here," replied the elf.

Overcome by weariness, I lay down on the floor of the cave. While the hard ground was not the most comfortable place to lay my head, it was far better than my previous accommodations, and I quickly fell into a deep, tranquil sleep.

I awoke the next morning feeling a little refreshed from my slumbers, stretching my arms over my head. It was good to be free.

"Ah, good! You're awake!" said a familiar voice. Vortimer sat by the fire, his little cauldron resting over the flame.

"Good morning," I said through a yawn. "I feel as though I have slept the sleep of the dead."

"You did sleep rather long."

"Where is the elf that was here?" I inquired.

"Off fetching breakfast. Ah, there he is now!"

Hefin entered the hollow, carrying a brace of fish in one hand and a pole in the other.

"Good to see you awake, my lord," said the elf.

"Mostly awake," I mumbled.

"You will feel more refreshed once you have some food in your belly. Will you kindly lend a hand, Vortimer?"

Vortimer and Hefin set about cooking the fish over the fire, talking of Tegid and Vortigern, and all that they were planning. They demonstrated a certain familiarity, as though they were friends, and I gathered that the two of them had been conspiring together for a great deal of time. There also seemed to be a strange excitement among them, like the two were celebrating a Christmas feast.

"I am afraid we must eat in haste," said Vortimer. "My father is combing the countryside. Not to mention Ceridwen and Tegid will have every beast of the mountains after you. We cannot stay in one place too long."

"Where shall we go, then?" I inquired.

"To Dyfed," replied Vortimer. "The king is a good man. He can help us."

"Can he take me back to Armorica?"

"You are not returning to Armorica," said Hefin.

I glared at the elf, confused. I had assumed that was the whole goal and end of this adventure: to return me to my family in Armorica.

"Events have been set in motion which cannot be interrupted now," he continued.

"Neither my father nor Tegid will relent until you are dead," added Vortimer. "He is jealous of his throne, and will destroy anyone who would dare challenge it. We must strike while the iron is hot! Take advantage of their confusion and restore the throne to its rightful owner."

"And how am I supposed to take back a kingdom without an army?"

"You will have an army," said Hefin. "There are thousands of men on this isle who have never bowed the knee to the old gods. They reject Vortigern and his false kingship, and would gladly march under the banner of the heir of King Custennin."

"Am I, though?"

"Are you what?" asked Hefin.

"The heir of King Custennin?" I replied, recalling what Vortimer told me.

Hefin furrowed his brow.

"What are you talking about?"

"Ceridwen divined through her forbidden arts that Custennin did not father Emrys," said Vortimer. There was an almost apologetic tone to his voice.

"Then who did?" asked Hefin, shocked.

"She did not reveal that."

"Then who am I?" I cried in desperation. "Why would anyone follow me if *I* do not even know who my father is?"

"Because they will know who *you* are," said Hefin.

Rising from his seat, Hefin drew a mighty longsword from its scabbard, and not just any longsword; this was the sword of Custennin. It was the same sword that the great kings of the West had carried into battle for a thousand generations, the sword that had been bathed in the blood of dragons before anyone knew the name of Rome. It was the same sword that Father let me hold as a young boy. I felt as though I could do anything holding that ancient sword in my small hands.

"Caledbur." I said the name reverently as I wrapped my fingers about the Atlantean steel. "How did you come by it?" I inquired. "I thought it lost."

"My people have been taking care of it for you," he replied. "Only the true king of the Brittons may wield it; you are the true king."

Solemnly, Hefin buckled the belt and scabbard about my waist while I admired the blade.

"Thank you, Sir Hefin," I said, sheathing the sword.

Hefin smiled. "It was my pleasure, good prince."

In that moment I realized the grim duty that lay before me; I was to put away boyish fears and take on the manly duties of saving the kingdom. The idea of more killing disgusted me, but it would be necessary for me to ascend the throne. It seems paradoxical to kill in the name of peace, but I had no choice. The land must be cleansed from Vortigern's sin.

5

After eating a hasty breakfast in the earthen hideaway, we gathered our meagre supplies and set out southward through the rugged, mist-veiled countryside.

Through the decaying archways and porticos of that long-forgotten metropolis we went. I marvelled at the massive stones and the unfathomable antiquity of it all.

"Hefin," I said, "what was this place? What used to be here?"

"Hyperborea; one of the city-states of old," replied the elf.

"What happened to it?"

"It was corrupted from its very foundation," he replied. "It fell before the combined forces of my ancestors and yours."

"Bala is all that is left," added Vortimer. "Would that *that* odious place had fallen, too."

The prince shuddered.

"You speak as though you have seen it," I said.

"I have been within its very walls."

I asked no more about it, as Vortimer seemed greatly disturbed, and I did not wish to trouble him further. Onward we trudged through that unforgiving country. My feet ached, though I grumbled not; complaining never accomplishes anything, and only draws attention to one's own ills. However, it is said that an army marches on its stomach and mine was becoming rather hollow.

"I do not wish to be a bother, Hefin," I began, "but it is well past midday and I think a meal would be of some benefit."

Reaching into his pack, Hefin drew out some fruit that resembled apples, tossing them to Vortimer and I.

"As Vortimer said, we must keep moving," he said. "We will stop at nightfall."

I nodded; it was a wise course of action, naturally.

I observed the fruit in my hand. It is said that these fruits grow wild on the isle of Avalon, and they are greatly beneficial. A man may march from dawn to dusk on but a single fruit. Indeed, they were quite good, having a flavor like honey, and I was quite satisfied after having eaten one. I marvelled at how the elves were so skilled to grow such fruits, and wondered why men were not able to cultivate them. Perhaps it was something in the soil of Avalon, or perhaps they knew some method of husbandry that had been lost in the subsequent ages between the fall of Atlantis and the rise of Rome. The elves are wary of explaining such things, and I kept my own council on the matter.

The light was beginning to fail as we set up camp within the crumbling remains of an ancient edifice. There were few trees in that place, the ground being hard and generally unyielding to their roots. As a result, Vortimer went rather far afield looking for wood, and what little wood we did find was damp from snow and mist.

"Blast it!" said Vortimer. "It is too damp; nothing will light!"

"Here," said Hefin, bending down to the wood. With a soft Elvish whisper, he conjured forth flames from the sticks.

"Thank you, Sir Hefin," said I.

"My pleasure, good prince."

We were indeed lucky to have such a magician on our side in this struggle. I doubt we would have survived that quest through the barren mountains without his skill.

Drawing a small bottle from his belt purse, Hefin sprinkled the contents in a wide circle about our camp.

"What are you doing?" I inquired.

"It is a salt circle," replied Hefin. "It will protect us from evil."

I nodded, thinking it odd that someone would carry so much salt and, furthermore, that they would waste such a valuable commodity pouring it out on the ground. But I did not voice such questions.

"I will take the first watch," I said, after we had supped.

"Nay, my lord," said Vortimer. "You should rest."

"You have worked hard enough this day, Vortimer," I replied. "You deserve the rest more than I do."

Vortimer assented, uttering his thanks. Untying his cloak from about his shoulders, he laid it on the ground and lay down on top of it. Hefin stayed awake, however.

"Will you not slumber, Hefin?" I asked.

"I will watch awhile," he replied. "There is evil abroad tonight. I think it best that you do not face it alone, at least for a time."

I nodded in agreement. Silently, we watched the flames, listening to the night beasts howling in the wilderness like the wailing of lost souls. It was an unnerving night; I marvelled how Vortimer could sleep so peacefully with the evil surrounding us. Perhaps he had just grown used to it. I feared I would lose my wits if I listened to that unholy noise any longer.

"What is an elf of Avalon doing in this God-forsaken country anyhow?" I inquired in the hope that conversation would stave off madness.

"It is for the very reason that God has *not* forsaken this country," he replied. "Everything has meaning and purpose. You must learn to see it."

"I am only the bastard prince of a half-forgotten kingdom on the edge of the civilized world," I retorted ruefully.

"Do not *ever* say that again!" rebuked Hefin. "A cosmic war is being fought, and every battle, no matter how small it may seem, is of infinite importance."

I looked wonderingly into the flames, considering all that Hefin had told me. If we did not stop them here, perhaps the gods would try to seize the continent next, maybe even Rome itself. Perhaps I was more important than I had previously thought.

Unearthly silence enveloped the whole wilderness. Each of my hairs stood on end. I felt the presence of something skulking in the dark, as though darkness itself had form and being. Yes, the Night was a living thing, and it watched us.

A wild, unnatural cry rent the stillness of the wilderness, waking Vortimer from his slumber, his eyes wide with fright.

"Put out the fire!" whispered Hefin.

Slowly drawing Caledbur from the scabbard, I crouched against the ancient stones, Hefin and Vortimer huddling close to me. Enormous feet crept through the snowy leaf litter, drawing nearer the threshold of the crumbling edifice. Whatever it was, it hunted us. I could practically smell its hot, putrid breath. Suddenly, the thing hissed like a serpent and retreated into the night, stirring the air with another hideous cry. I sighed, relieved the thing had wandered off.

The sense of unease would not lift, however; the Night was still watching. I kept my watch until Vortimer took my place half-way through the dark hours, and fell into a restless slumber.

6

I emerged from sleep to the smell of roasted meat, feeling little-rested and quite ravenous. Vortimer turned a fowl on a spit over the fire, humming softly to himself.

"Good morning, my lord," he greeted me.

"Good morning," I replied.

"Sleep well?" he inquired.

"I caught a few winks," I replied.

"I certainly did not," replied Vortimer.

"What was that... thing?" I asked.

"We are better off not knowing. I have seen some of the beings Ceridwen and Tegid breed in the pits of Bala, and I wish that I had not."

Vortimer shuddered. I thought it best to change the subject.

"Where has Hefin gone to?" I inquired.

"He went off to scout ahead."

"That is a bit dangerous, is it not?"

"Not for him," said Vortimer. "Hefin can make himself invisible, or nearly so, if he desires."

I nodded. Hefin, it seemed to me, knew more of wood-craft than the beasts themselves. The lore of the forest was as natural to him as walking.

"Ah, there he is now," said Vortimer, gesturing.

Hefin ran into the camp like a hunted stag, his face pale with dread.

"What is the matter?" I inquired.

"Hengist and his men are approaching!" panted Hefin.

Vortimer cursed.

"What shall we do?" I asked in desperation.

"I have an idea," said Vortimer. "Hide, both of you."

Without another word, I followed Hefin to a nearby cleft in the rock where we concealed ourselves. The cleft afforded us some protection, but little room; we barely fit. There we waited, barely breathing, as the horses' hooves beat relentlessly on the hard earth. The Saxons halted their horses as Vortimer greeted them.

"Prince Vortimer," said Hengist. "Your father's been looking for you."

"I have been searching for Emrys," replied Vortimer.

"Good lad," said Hengist. "So have we. We think he may be headed southward."

"That would make sense," replied Vortimer. "King Kynyr has never been on friendly terms with my father; Emrys would find safety there."

Following our scent, the hounds sniffed the ground, drawing nearer and nearer the cleft. I am loath to kill a dog; they are but beasts, after all, and have no rational will and no malice. However, if they were to threaten us, I would have little choice but to end their lives. Thus I grasped Caledbur's hilt, ready to draw it should the need arise.

"Well, come then, mount up!" said Hengist. He then barked an order in Saxon. "Perhaps we can catch him if we ride together."

A soft, almost inaudible Elvish whisper came from Hefin's lips. As if in answer, the hounds let out a loud howl, fleeing into the wilderness. With a loud grunt, Hengist and his men beat a trail through the wild after the dogs. Relieved, Hefin and I exhaled a deep sigh.

As soon as the hoof beats faded away, we emerged from our hiding place.

"How did you do that?" I inquired.

"I told the hounds to lead them away."

"You are full of surprises!" I chuckled.

"You have no idea," he replied, smiling enigmatically.

After a hasty breakfast, we broke camp and made our way southward, being careful to avoid the path of Hengist and his men. Hefin assured me that he had commanded the dogs to take them away from our trail, and furthermore, that Vortimer would do his very best to prevent our capture.

We kept to the valleys and glens to avoid being spied on the mountains. Through the deeps we went, meandering our way toward Dyfed, or at least I hoped so. I began to wonder if Hefin were just as lost as I was.

"Hefin," I said at last. "Are we any nearer to Dyfed?"

"Yes, of course we are. Where do you think I have been taking you?"

"It seems to me that we have been going in circles. I know I have seen that rock before. And look; those are my footprints."

Hefin furrowed his brows in confusion; I could even read a bit of anxiety behind his expression. He ran his fingers through his dark hair.

"It is these cursed mountains!" he exclaimed. "They are bewitched!"

He sat down on a large stone, holding his head in his hands.

"Take heart," I said. "I am certain we will find the way to Dyfed soon."

"This never should have happened," moaned Hefin.

"Well, it is happening now, and we must make do with it," I replied.

"I should not even be here. I was never prepared for this."

"If you had not been there, then surely I would have been sacrificed to the gods. All this is a small part of a larger plan, as you said. Now, the night is falling. We should gather some kindling wood and make camp."

"Alright," said Hefin with a slight smile.

Having gathered the wood, we sat down to a rather pleasant fire we had built under a rocky outcrop. There was again that feeling of being observed.

"I meant that, you know," said Hefin. "My father, King Nudd forbade me from interfering in the affairs of man's realm, but I could no longer stand by and watch."

"I understand."

"I never thought I would even meet the high king, let alone rescue him. I was just spying."

"Well, you appear to be rather good at it."

He smiled. "You shall make a good king, should we survive this."

"We will," I said with a wry smile. "It would be a pity to come all this way just to die in the wilderness. That would leave my brother in charge. Heaven help us if that happened!"

Hefin laughed. There was a strange music to his laughter, like a babbling brook.

"I hope *my* brother is alright. We were out hunting when I was captured, you see. Hopefully he found his way back to Uncle Aldrien's fortress without me."

"He is probably more concerned about you."

"Indeed," I replied. "We are brothers, but more than that, we are friends. He must be devastated."

Hefin sighed. "Would that my brother and I were that close."
"Oh?"

"Prince Gwyn and I are rather far apart in ages, you see."

"I do not even know how old you are," I remarked.

"I shall pass my fifth winter by the reckoning of Avalon."

I narrowed my eyes at the youth.

"You seem very mature for a boy of five," I said with a chuckle.

"Winter does not occur so often there," he replied. "I am uncertain how old I am in the reckoning of men, though I presume we are about equal."

"I have heard that elves live many lifetimes of men; how long will you live?"

He paused for a moment. "If my strength endures, I shall live to be about six thousand years of men."

I could hardly fathom living for so many centuries.

7

Hefin insisted on taking the first watch, and I did not argue. I felt as though I could no longer keep my own eyes open; it would be futile to attempt to remain awake.

This weariness would not relent, however; even after some hours of sound sleep, I was still fatigued when my watch came. I am ashamed to admit I dozed off half-way through my vigil. But I did not remain that way for long.

Shortly after, I was awakened by the sound of something rifling through our bags. At the edge of camp, what appeared to be a young child rummaged in our provisions. There was something not quite right about it.

"Hello there," I said to the little creature, who gave a slight yelp and vanished into the dark. I immediately gave chase; I did not even know why at the time. It simply seemed to be the proper thing to do.

"Do not be afraid," I called into the blackness. "I am not here to hurt you."

Silence answered my calling. I could only hope that nothing worse than a lost child had heard me. Discouraged at my own foolishness, I turned about and started back for camp. Unfortunately, I seemed to have lost my way. Breathing a curse into the dark, I began attempting to retrace my steps. This proved impossible, however, as dawn was still some time off. Just as I was about to give up hope of finding camp again, I saw a speck of light some way off. Believing it to be our campfire, I followed the light through the stygian wilderness. Suddenly, I felt the earth give way beneath me. Not wishing to give myself away, I stifled a shout as I fell into a deep pit.

I felt the sides of the pit with my fingers; there seemed to be no means of climbing, at least, not easily. I did not wish to call, as someone would likely be listening. I could only hope that Hefin would eventually come searching for me and find me down here.

There comes a time in every man's life when he must look things squarely in the face and take stock of everything that has happened. I had been kidnapped and taken to Britain, nearly sacrificed to evil gods, lost, cold, alone in a hole. *But I still live,* I thought. This was true; I was not dead, and life was still sweet to me, despite all my trials.

I looked up at the sky above me. The stars twinkled through the wispy clouds, and I could just see the rays of dawn gathering in the east.

Soon, Hefin would come looking for me. He was quite the experienced tracker, and would surely find me here.

A moment later, I perceived the outline of a small face looking down into the hole

"Hello down there!" called a voice from above.

"Hello," I replied, quizzically. "What are you doing here?"

"I might ask you the same question, big fella," he retorted.

"Can you get me out of this hole?"

"Yes, I can," replied the child. "Do I want to? That's a different question."

My confusion grew greater. Why would he not want to help me? Was he some sort of spy for Vortigern, or Ceridwen? Was this a trap laid for me?

"My companion will come looking for me," I said sharply. "He will be quite cross if you do not help me out of this hole!"

"Oh, I'd like to help you," said the child, "but I'd also like a few coins to rub together."

"I have no money to give you," I replied.

"Yeah, I figured that out," responded the child, ruefully.

"Were you the one rifling through our bags?"

"You guessed it, handsome!"

"I have nothing to offer you as payment, but I simply must get out of this hole!"

"You gotta have *some* valuables," he retorted. "That's a dandy sword. Could fetch a good price at Dwarf Market."

"I would sooner surrender my life than this sword!" I snapped.

"Well, have a nice death!"

"Wait a minute!" I growled. "I am a prince. I will soon be high king. Perhaps if you let me out of here, we can work out some form of compensation later."

A long silence ensued. I was beginning to become impatient with this rather impetuous child.

"Oh, hey there," said the child. "Your friend is down in the hole. Whoa, let's not get too hasty! Put that thing away. He's fine, just feeling a little hollow right now."

"Are you alright, good prince?" asked the voice of Hefin.

"I am well, Hefin" I replied.

"Here, have a rope," said the child as a rope descended from above. Taking hold of the rope, I climbed up to the surface, where Hefin and the child waited. I became aware, in the gathering daylight, that this was not a child at all; it was a very small woman. she had the proportions of a grown adult but her head only coming to about the height of my waist. Her skin was a blueish-grey hue. Large, pointed ears protruded through her long, straight, red-brown hair. She wore a tunic and trousers like a man, which were rather drab and ragged-looking.

She stood there, leaning on a poleaxe that seemed far too long for her. By her side was a grey-colored goat, saddled like a small horse with various bags and supplies loaded on its back.

"Now," I said, once I had reached the mouth of the pit, "who, or *what* are you?"

"I'm Willamina," replied the creature with a little curtsey. "I'm a hobgoblin."

The little people of the wilderness were not unknown in those days, though few had seen them. It is said they are quite good at hiding their presence.

"Why did you trap me?"

"Figured you must have some coin on you," shrugged the hobgoblin. "Guess I was wrong."

I scowled.

"Hey, a girl's gotta eat. Here's an idea: you two seem kinda lost; how would you like a guide?"

"We can find our own way, thank you," I replied.

"My lord," said Hefin, drawing me aside. "I think we should use her."

"But she might be some sort of spy!" whispered.

"The gods have been trying to exterminate the hobgoblins for generations. They are thieves, but they are relatively harmless. She might be able to help us get to Dyfed."

"I suppose it would be better to have her as an ally than an enemy," I admitted.

Turning back toward Willamina, I said: "We would appreciate your services as a guide, however, we have no means of compensating you at this time."

"Well, you are a prince after all. I'm sure you've got gobs of money back in your castle. Besides that, the Witch-Queen is out for your hide. That's good enough for me."

The diminutive woman mounted the goat.

"Come on! We'll have breakfast at my place before we head to Dyfed."

8

Willamina led us through the dawning wilderness to a small hut built low in the earth. So low, in fact, that I would have missed it entirely had she not pointed out the entrance.

Undoing the goat's saddle and bags, the diminutive maid opened the little door in the side of the hut and led us inside. It was rather difficult to stand upright (even as a youth, I was tall in stature) but it was a pleasant place.

"It ain't much, but it's home," said the hobgoblin, as she hung her coat upon a stag horn that served as a coat rack. She then untied her pointed boots and placed them near the fireplace, inviting us to do the same.

"Lemme fix you something to eat. Make yourselves at home!"

We took our seats on small stools while Willamina set about making a meal with whatever provisions she had.

"So you're high king, eh?" asked the hobgoblin. "Everyone thought you and your brother were dead. Where have you been?"

"I have spent the last ten years with my Uncle Aldrien in Armorica."

"And you're back to dethrone King Full-Of-Himself?"

"Something like that, yes. He tried to have me killed, and would have, had not Hefin saved me."

"That's why the witch is after you, I bet," said the hobgoblin as she placed bowls of stew before us.

"I robbed her of her prize," said Hefin.

"And what a prize it is, too!"

I was not accustomed then to being complimented in such a manner, and flushed somewhat at her remark.

"You think you can actually win?" asked the hobgoblin.

"I am certain of it," I replied.

"Lots of luck!"

"You sound as though you do not believe we can do it," remarked Hefin.

"Let's face the facts; Vortigern has all the forces of Bala on his side and you have... a sword."

"It is more than just a sword," I protested. "It is Caledbur, slayer of monsters."

"It's gonna be awfully busy once you get to the actual fighting."

"I shall expect nothing less."

"Will you still guide us to Dyfed?" asked Hefin.

"I didn't say I wouldn't, but don't ask me to come to your funeral."

"You are rather impertinent," I remarked.

"All hobgoblins are," she replied. "Honesty is one of our most treasured virtues."

"Yet you are a thief."

"An honest thief."

"How can one be an 'honest thief'?"

"I didn't hide the fact that I was trying to rob you. Now, Vortigern, he's a dishonest thief; he'll take your stuff, but under the pretense of protecting you, except he has no intention of actually protecting anyone other than himself, but he doesn't want you to know that."

Hefin and I chuckled; she had a rather good point and an amusing way of making it. Once we had finished our breakfast, we gathered a few supplies for the remainder of the journey and left the little hut. Willamina placed two fingers in her mouth and blew a shrill whistle.

"Billy! Come here you old goat!" she called.

Around a hillock came the goat that served as her steed, bleating happily. Placing the saddle and bags upon his back, Wallamina mounted the beast.

"And away we go!" she said cheerfully.

We followed the maiden and goat into the frosty wilds, heading on a meandering route southwards toward the kingdom of Dyfed. The sun peeked through the clouds; it felt like it had been months since I had seen its shining face last. It seemed as though all the howling beasts of the mountains had hidden themselves from its rays; their wild cries ceased, being replaced by the gentle songs of birds.

"Huh," said Willamina. "First time in years I've heard anything other than carrion crows in the mountains. Weird."

"Do you know what they are singing about?" asked Hefin.

"No," I replied.

"They are singing because the king is come to put things right again."

I felt strangely warmed by his words. Or perhaps it was the feeling of spring stirring in the wind. Puddles formed on the hard, rocky earth as the snow melted. This made our journey a bit more challenging, but we had become accustomed to challenges by now.

"This place seems not fit for man nor beast," I remarked. "What made you choose to live here?"

"Well, hobgoblins ain't exactly the most popular creatures. We tend to live in places where big folk leave us alone. Of course, if you give us a place to lay our heads and a meal to eat, we'll make sure your place is spick and span."

"That is very kind of you, considering," I replied.

The maiden shrugged. "Better than being chased from pillar to post. We don't want to make trouble for anyone, but we need food and a roof over our heads just like anyone else."

"I have never understood why they hate you so much," added Hefin.

"Same here, princess."

I thought that it was peculiar that Willamina referred to Hefin as "princess". She did so several times, and I thought it some sort of crude jest, but said nothing, since Hefin made no retort.

Willamina continued, "We used to live in peace with the big folk, but that was a long time ago. Not sure what happened."

Her tale was a sorrowful one, and I could not help but feel sympathy for the plight of the little folk. I resolved then and there to do them no injustice whenever I should meet one of their kind.

By mid-day we came to a wide, babbling stream. Willamina paused on the bank, looking left and right.

"Dyfed's just over there." said the hobgoblin, pointing at a pass between two mountains.

"I suppose we shall have to wade across," I said. I did not relish the thought of stepping into the ice-cold waters, but it seemed to be the only way to get to Dyfed. I therefore bent down to unlace my boots.

"Wait a minute," said Willamina. "We have to ask permission."

The calm waters stirred, as though a large fish were swimming in the current. Out of the stream came what appeared to be a beautiful woman, pulling herself onto a large rock protruding from the water. I soon realized that this was no ordinary woman at all; from the waist up, she appeared human, but where her legs ought to be was the long, scaly tail of a fish. This was none other than a nixie: a maiden of the river.

"What is it you want, Willamina, daughter of Mudbert?"

"We want to cross the river, if you'd be so kind as to let us, Lady Delyth."

"Who are your companions?" asked the nixie.

"I am Emrys, the true High King of Britain. This is my companion, Hefin of Avalon."

"High King, eh?"

Delyth descended from her perch and swam to the shore where we stood waiting to cross. Drawing herself out of the cold waters, she sat upright on the stony bank nearest me, leaning to one side. She was quite lovely to look at; long sleek black hair, smooth, pale skin, full lips, and glistening silver eyes. I looked deeply into those shining irises, transfixed, unable to look away.

"There is no guile within you," said the nixie. "No deception. You are the true king."

"Will you allow us to cross, then?" I asked.

She turned her attention to Hefin. "You, on the other hand, are not all you seem to be."

I looked at Hefin; the elf was inscrutable. My mind whirled with wild speculation as to what he might be hiding from me. Was he leading me to a trap? Was he a spy for Vortigern?

"Do not fear, fair prince," said Delyth at last. "It is of little consequence. I will allow you to cross, but the elf must pay a toll. Something very precious."

Hefin's expression soured. Reaching into his pouch, he drew forth a necklace of exquisite workmanship. He tossed this rather feminine-looking jewelry to the nixie, who immediately put it about her neck.

"You may cross now."

The waters parted like the Red Sea of Scripture, and we walked across on dry ground.

"Thanks a million, Delyth!" said Willamina.

"Have a care, good prince," said the nixie. "It is a hard road you travel."

I nodded my head to the lady as the waters filled the riverbed again.

Tears rolled down Hefin's face. "That necklace belonged to my mother," he whispered.

"I am very sorrowful for you," I said. Indeed, my heart grew heavy for him. It seemed he paid a very high price just to accompany me on this endeavor; perhaps too high. I felt as though I owed him an even greater debt than I had before.

"It was worth it," said the elf, wiping his eyes. "She would have considered it worth the price."

I replied not; more often than not, it is better to grieve in silence, rather than to speak or to be spoken to.

9

    The sun receded below the horizon, making way for another night in those deplorable mountains. I wondered if I should ever escape that hellish place alive. The wicked eyes of Ceridwen rested their hateful gaze on us. Everywhere and nowhere at once her presence could be felt, like a serpent in the reeds.

    I placed my hand on Caledbur, holding the pommel tightly. Gradually, a feeling of peace washed over me, like holding my father's hand again, his strong presence walking with me in the night. I would need that strength to get me through the next trial.

    Willamina, conversely, seemed either oblivious or heedless of any dangers in the gathering darkness. She sung a merry tune as she rode her goat through the wilderness.

"The fox went out on a chilly night.

He prayed for the moon to give him light,

For he'd many a mile to go that night

Before he'd reach the town-o, town-o, town-o.

He'd many a mile to go that night before he'd reach the town-o."

"Willamina," I began, "why is it you sing such a merry song in this dreadful place, especially as the night is falling?"

"It's the best way to defy the witch," she replied. "Singing a cheerful song, especially when the night is falling, tells her you ain't afraid of her and her devils."

"Joy, cheer, merriment; these are the greatest weapons against the darkness," added Hefin.

Seeing the wisdom in their words, I put on a cheerful countenance and began a happy song I had heard in Armorica. From that day forward, this philosophy has kept me stalwart and brave through many evils and will hopefully keep me through many more.

A sudden thunderous crack interrupted our singing as a large boulder flew into our path. Another followed it, just missing my head. All about us, like a demonic choir, low bellowing cries such as I had never heard before in all my life filled the night.

"Trolls!" cried Willamina. "Time to beat feet!"

We took to our heels as more large rocks hurtled through the air all about us like a rain of death. However, we would not escape so easily. Like a fisherman's net, the creatures closed in about us, their large, misshapen forms silhouetted in the fading light. Willamina let out a curse. Hefin drew his weapons. I pulled the Atlantean steel from the scabbard.

In my boyhood, I had heard about trolls, but I thought them to be wives' tales intended to frighten young children into behaving. How wrong I was about so many things!

I cut deeply into the belly of the first troll that approached. The dying troll let out a low moan, dropping to the earth with a heavy thud. From my immediate right came a club-wielding monster, raring back for a broad, sweeping strike. In one fluid motion, I ducked the blow, severed the club-hand, and sliced through the monster's gut.

Any fear I felt before vanished like smoke in the heat of battle. I was an instrument of destruction; the only thought in my mind was victory.

For being so small of stature, Willamina managed to make a good account of herself, fighting with the fierceness of a warrior thrice her size. She rode her steed in and out between the legs of creatures, who were too slow and stupid to notice the diminutive fighter. Her poleaxe never ceased from chopping into their legs.

Hefin, meanwhile, wielding a strange elvish weapon, shot what looked like lightning and fire at the creatures, burning them and sending some squealing for the hills like frightened swine.

The thunder of horses' hooves shook the glen. Into the trolls' thick skin flew spears and arrows. The injured and dying beasts cried out, dripping black blood from their wounds as they retreated into the gloom.

"Aye! Run, ya devils!" cried the voice of a man.

Our saviors circled their horses about us. A young man who appeared to be their chieftain pointed his spear at me. He was older than myself, and broader. His hair and beard were of a flaming red hue, and his skin was ruddy and freckled. Every part of him was muscular.

"Now," said the war-leader, "who be ye, and what are ye doing on our borders?"

"Surely your eyes have not failed you, King Kynyr," said Hefin.

"Hefin!" the horseman cried gladly. Leaping down from his steed, he clapped the youth heartily on the back.

"Good to see you again, mate! Keeping an eye on the usurper still?"

"Indeed, good king," said Hefin.

"And who be this, then?" asked Kynyr, gesturing in my direction.

"The one we have been hoping for," replied Hefin.

"The heir?" said Kynyr, squinting skeptically at me.

"Yes, I am he," I replied. "I am Emrys, son of Custennin."

"And the future high king," added Hefin.

A wry smile replaced Kynyr's skepticism, and suddenly I was enveloped in his mighty arms.

"They told me I was mad for thinking you were still alive, yet here you are!"

Kynyr released me from his embrace, saying: "Come! Let's take ye back to Caer Goch! Here, ye can ride my horse."

"That is hardly necessary," I protested.

"Bah! I insist! What sort of king would I be if I let the future high king of Britain walk all the way back to the fort?"

"Very well," I assented, not wishing to insult the man's honor.

It was about that time that I realized that our guide had vanished.

"Hefin," I said, "where is Willamina?"

"More likely than not, she has disappeared into the wilderness. Hobgoblins do not care to be around so many of the big folk, especially those with horses. She will return to collect payment someday."

I nodded. I would never forget the kindness she had shown us in our time of greatest need, and I would make sure that she was more than adequately compensated should I see her again.

Together, King Kynyr and I rode at the front of the band, leading them southwest toward Caer Goch, the seat of power in Dyfed.

10

"Make way for the high king!" shouted Kynyr as we approached the high stone walls of Caer Goch. With a loud creaking of hinges, the timber gates opened wide for us. Quizzical looks met the sight of a stranger on their king's own horse, but Kynyr demanded obeisance from his men, and they would not defy him. Kynyr, despite his youth and inexperience, was a great warrior, and highly respected by all in Dyfed. He was a man of reckless courage who led his troops by example.

Caer Goch, being farther away from the more Romanized Londinium and Camelot, is mostly constructed of timber, rather than stone or Roman concrete. Most of the houses have the thatched roofs found on more traditional British homes. The people there are of a more British character as well, being tall and lean with swarthy skin and dark, curly hair. Like their ancestors before them, men of Dyfed do not shave their upper lips.

We rode toward the great house to much pomp as peasants and warriors congratulated the king for his success in repelling the denizens of the darkness.

"Come!" said Kynyr. "Ye must be famished from your travels; let us get ye some food."

"I would welcome it," I replied.

To the great mead hall of Caer Goch we went, where his servants awaited their king's command.

"Morgwen!" called the king to his servant. "Bread! Cheese! Beer! A joint of meat, if there is any!"

The servants obliged the master of the house, bringing us food and drinks while we took our seats at the table. King Kynyr reclined in his great oaken chair with his left leg hooked over the armrest, looking as jolly and cheerful as any king could be. I sat to his right, and Hefin across the table from me.

As nourishing as Hefin's elf fruit was, stewed meat and good wine were a welcome refreshment. It is necessary for a king and a warrior to be accustomed to the privations of the road and the assaults of nature, but one must also enjoy the fine things in life: good food, warm fires, songs and fellowship.

"Tell me, Kynyr," I requested, "how is it that Dyfed has not been invaded?"

"I have a special arrangement with Lord Arawn," replied the king, casually taking a draught from his drinking horn. "An ancestor of mine, King Pwyll, did Lord Arawn a favor, so Arawn forbade the gods from ever meddling in Dyfed, but that doesn't keep Vortigern or Tegid from trying. That's why me men and I are always patrolling the border."

Kynyr took another draught of beer.

"How about yourself?" he asked. "Where have ye been these past years, and what are ye doing back?"

"My mother took Uther and me to live in Armorica with my uncle," I replied. "Vortigern had me kidnapped and brought to the mountains for one of his profane sacrifices."

"Sounds about right; heathen berk!" spat the king of Dyfed. "What do you plan to do about the usurper?"

"I do not know yet," I replied. "We do not have the manpower to attack him outright, do we?"

"Do not worry about that, good prince," replied the Red King. "There are thousands of men in Britain who reject Vortigern and his false kingship. Once they hear the true king has returned, you'll have your army."

Hope sprang up in my spirit. "We'll send that blaggard back to hell where he belongs! How soon can you muster your troops?"

"All I have to do is say the word!"

"So be it," I replied. "We ride tomorrow!"

"Excellent!" said Kynyr, clapping his hands.

The king gestured to the servants, signalling them to clear the dirty dishes from the table. They then led us to our accommodations, where we retired for the night. Exhausted, I fell into a deep sleep the moment I lay down on the soft bed.

I awoke early the next morning, rested and refreshed, the first time I had felt so since my unwanted departure from Armorica. I stretched my arms, still sore from our battle with the trolls, yawning deeply before rising from my bed and dressing for the day.

The midwinter morning was bright and crisp as I made my way to the chapel for morning prayers. I thought it best to prepare myself spiritually before the coming battle, and to thank the Almighty for the many deliverances He had wrought for me in my travails. Certainly His blessing was upon me, otherwise I most surely would have perished in the wilderness.

Entering the house of worship, I made the sign of the Cross, and knelt before the altar to pray. However, I was not alone in the chapel; the sound of hushed voices nearby interrupted my supplication.

"I know you do not approve," said one voice, "but this is too important!"

There was a familiarity to that voice, and in a moment I realized that it was none other than Hefin.

"My lady," said another voice, "it is not for me to approve or disapprove, but the Lord is not a God of falsehood!"

"Even if it is in the service of justice?" pleaded Hefin.

The man sighed. "It was all well and good when you were simply spying on Vortigern and the Saxons, but you have lied to the future *high king of Britain*! What will happen if he finds out?"

"You would not tell him, Deacon Dubric?"

"It is not mine to tell, my lady."

My lady? I thought. Why would he address him thus? My mind went back to the day before when the nixie had prevented Hefin from crossing the river on account of a secret he was keeping. I had noticed that

Hefin had a feminine look, but I thought it was due to the fact that he was an elvish youth. Could it be that he - or she - had deceived me?

In the midst of my musings, the deacon entered the chapel, accompanied by the elf I called Hefin.

"Good morning, sire," said the deacon.

"Good morning, deacon," I replied.

"Good morning, prince," said Hefin.

"Good morning," I returned, hesitantly.

"What troubles you, my lord?" he - or she - inquired.

"Just thinking about the battle," I said, not wanting to reveal that I had been eavesdropping.

Hefin nodded. "I have faith we shall prevail against the adversary."

"As do I," I replied. "We could not have come this far without it."

"Now you understand," replied the elf with a smile.

We then entered the silence of prayer. I asked the Almighty for wisdom to know how I should approach the coming battle; while Hefin, or whatever her name was, was a fine warrior, I did not think it proper for a lady to enter the fighting; still she (if indeed the elf was "she") was a fine warrior of great skill and daring, and I was loath to dismiss her outright. It is improper for a king to eavesdrop, after all, and I did not wish to embarrass her either. These thoughts were troublesome enough that I simply could not concentrate on my prayers.

After a lengthy period of prayer and a reading from the Psalms, we left the chapel. I had been too distracted to notice that King Kynyr had joined us in the chapel. The red king approached us, grinning.

"So," began Kynyr, "when do we get to beat some Saxon arse?"

"We may leave as soon as we are ready," I replied, chuckling.

"Alright then!" said Kynyr with a hearty laugh. "Let's get you some armor!"

Leading us to the armory, the king of Dyfed had us outfitted with the accoutrements of war. I peered over at Hefin, wondering if now was the right time to ask.

"What is it?" asked Hefin with a quizzical expression.

"Nothing," I replied. "Just preparing for the battle."

Hefin laughed. "Still? We are on the eve of war, my lord. Now is not the time for second thoughts."

"Come then!" cried Kynyr, boisterously. "Let's get the horses and ride out!"

The warriors of Dyfed raised a great shout, singing a song of war as they marched out of the armory.

Once the war band was mounted and assembled we rode through the streets of Caer Goch, the thunderous applause of peasants cheering us on. Indeed, it was an awesome sight, the flags and banners of Dyfed fluttering in the winter wind, the martial splendor of the fighting men in their glittering coats of mail and shining helmets, their long spears and pikes resting on their brawny shoulders.

Through the gates we rode, King Kynyr and I at the head of the band, and made our way eastward toward Londinium.

11

A strange uneasiness weighed on us as we rode through the snow and frost. A dark shape glided through the wood, following our every move. While it appeared to be a carrion crow, there was something otherworldly about it; it was likely one of Ceridwen's spies, if not Ceridwen herself. It is known that she has mastered many shapes.

I saw also the shapes of many human figures dashing in and out among the trees.

"Halt!" I commanded.

We stood motionless among the trees, watching and waiting for any sound or movement.

"What is it, Emrys?" asked Kynyr.

"We are being followed," I replied.

"By whom?"

"I am uncertain."

"They are not our foes," said Hefin.

Out the forest came men armed with spear and bow. A tall man approached me, drawing back his green hood.

"Who do you think you are, eh?" asked Kynyr. "Highwaymen? Or perhaps some of Vortigern's crew?"

"Nay," said the tall, grave man. "We owe no allegiance to the pretender. We are outlaws; here by our own choice. Who are you, then, my lord?"

"I am Kynyr, King of Dyfed, and this is Emrys, the future High King."

The outlaw looked incredulous. "High King? But I heard all of Custennin's heirs were dead."

"Well, I am not dead," I said, drawing Caledbur from its sheath. "Let us pass, or you shall know the might of Caledbur."

"I had heard rumors among the peasants that you had returned, but I thought they were nothing more."

"Well, ye thought wrong!" cried Kynyr. "Now make way!"

"My lords," said the outlaw, "we have come here to this wood to escape the tyranny of Vortigern, and are skilled in the ways of battle. If you will allow us, we would gladly pledge ourselves to the service of the true king."

The outlaw knelt down before me, bowing his head, as did the other outlaws with him.

"What is your name?" I inquired.

"I am called Gorlois," replied the outlaw.

"Rise, Gorlois," I said. "We are going to Londinium to put an end to the usurper. You will march with us."

The outlaws took their places among the men at arms, marching behind us as we continued on toward Londinium and our journey's end.

Toward evening, we stopped in a forest glade, where we pitched our camp to spend the night. There we sat about our campfires, talking, jesting and eating. Gorlois and his men were stalwart fellows; some were commoners, others were noblemen who had had their lands seized. In spite of this, they treated one another as equals. They were all victims of Vortigern's tyranny, and they all lived in hope that one day he would be overthrown. Their captain was something of a mystery; none knew from where he came, whether he was of noble or common blood, or how he had come to be an outlaw. All anyone knew was that he lived in the forest and hated Vortigern and all his devilry.

I said little that evening; my mind was more occupied with Hefin's true identity. Who really was this elf that had led me to safety? What else might he - or she? - be hiding?

I bristled when the elf sat down next to me with a bowl of pottage.

"Sire," inquired Hefin, "are you well? You have barely said a thing since we left Caer Goch."

"Not much else to say, I suppose," I replied. I tried futilely to hide the angry edge to my voice.

"Very well," said Hefin. "You may continue lying to me if you wish."

"I might say the same," I retorted.

Hefin shot me a fiery glance. "What do you mean by that?"

"At the river, the nixie said you were hiding something."

Hefin's countenance paled. "It is unimportant."

"It was important enough to prevent your crossing," I retorted.

The elf sighed. "Follow me."

I followed Hefin a short distance from the camp, out of earshot of the war band.

"I confess that I have not been entirely truthful, my prince," he said. "My name is not Hefin; it is Nimue, and I am princess of Avalon."

I breathed a sigh of relief. Finally, I knew with certainty. Everything seemed to make sense, and I no longer had to ponder what it was she concealed from me.

"Why did you not tell me?" I questioned.

"I had to disguise myself as a male to spy on Vortigern. I feared that if you found out I was a maid, you would not let me help you, and I desperately wanted to help you."

Nimue looked at the ground, nervously fumbling with the end of her belt. My mind reeled. Many things about her seemed to fall into place; her appearance, why Willamina referred to her as "princess", the necklace at the river. I felt embarrassed, as though I had done her injury; it is improper to treat a lady as one treats a man, after all. I wondered if Vortimer knew, and if he did, what the true nature of their friendship was. I did not wish for her to enter the fighting, but I also did not wish for her to depart our company entirely. However, an idea did occur to me. I placed a hand on her slender shoulder.

"Perhaps we can use you to greater effect," I said.

Nimue lifted her head, eyes full of hope.

"I believe I have a plan," I added, smiling.

12

The king paused in his tale, taking a draught of wine.

"This part of the tale is equally important," said Emrys, "but I fear I shall not tell it aright. "

Emrys turned his head to look at his queen.

"Dear wife, would you oblige us by telling the tale in your own words?"

"Certainly!" replied Nimue. She then told the next portion of the tale as follows.

* * *

Saxon mercenaries stood on the city gates of Londinium, leaning lazily on their long spears as the sun took his leave in the west. They took no notice of me bobbing and weaving between bits of shrubbery, creeping my way along the walls like a mouse, my grey cloak blending with the grey light of eventide.

The walls of Londinium had fallen into a state of disrepair since the Romans' departure decades earlier, and there were many gaps and cracks where it had been damaged by the ravages of weather and time. It took no time at all for me to find one of these cracks and squeeze inside. Living in the wild for nearly a year had molded my frame, making it lean and nimble.

Through the narrow streets I snaked, taking note of everything I saw. Barely anything stirred in those twilight hours, save for a few animals nosing amongst the urban refuse. There is a certain pleasure I have discovered in sneaking and spying; the thrill of being right near one's enemy and yet being unseen. There is nothing I can liken it to. My heart beat a bit faster as I made my way toward the middle of the city.

Drawing near to the Great House, I heard the voices of men shouting in the Cumbric language within its walls; being an elf, I have much stronger hearing than an ordinary man. Crouching down near one of the windows, I listened attentively to what was being said.

"I have had my fill of your lies, old man!" shouted a voice which I recognised from many months of spying: Vortigern.

"God will not be mocked, Vortigern," replied a powerful, but unfamiliar voice. "Repent of your devilry and return to the Lord. He will have mercy on you."

"I have no need of your hanging god, Germanus!" roared Vortigern. "My gods have given me everything: kingdom, lands, wealth, armies; what has your god given you?"

"Eternal life," replied the man named Germanus. "You have sold your soul for a mere pot of stew!"

"I am king of Britain!"

"A trifle!"

"You are nothing but an old fool!"

"God hath made the foolish things of this world to put to shame the wise," quoth Germanus. "I urge you, Vortigern. Repent! Or you shall surely burn!"

"Cerdic, show this doddard out of my house."

"The Lord rebuke you!" cried Germanus as a Saxon mercenary escorted him from the dwelling. Moments later, there was a heavy *thud* followed by a grunt as the mercenary tossed Germanus into the courtyard. There was a long silence after that. I was about to leave, when I heard another voice, that of Vortimer.

"I have returned, father," he said.

"Ah, Vortimer," replied the usurper. "Have you found the bastard?"

"Alas, I have not," replied the prince. "We searched those hills high and low. It must have been some sort of magic."

"Surely you could have come upon some remnant of him," said Vortigern.

"The cold or the beasts probably got him," said a deep, hoarse voice in a heavy Saxon accent.

"But they did not," said a voice, cold with malice; surely a voice I knew, but could not name where I heard it. A chill ran down my spine whenever it spoke.

"Praise be to Ceridwen, mistress of life and death," said the usurper. I shuddered at the mention of that name.

"The boy king still lives," said the evil queen. "He comes now with a war-band of Dyfed to these very gates."

I knew that she had been watching us, but somehow it still galled me that she warned Vortigern of our approach.

"We shall repel them easily, surely," the usurper scoffed.

"Be not overly confident, Vortigern," continued Ceridwen. "The lad is strong of courage, and of great skill. Furthermore, there is a traitor among us: your very own son."

There was a long pause. My heart sank. Vortimer had become a dear friend to me; what would become of him now that his secret was known?

"Is this true, Vortimer?" queried Vortigern.

Another long pause followed.

"Yes, Father," replied Vortimer. "I will no longer stand idly by while you continue to commit abominations. You and your detestable religion can go to the Pit!"

I was quite proud of Vortimer in that moment. Ever since I had met him, he had been afraid to defy his father to his face, and now he finally said what was on his noble heart.

"Blasphemy!" cried Vortigern. "Hengist, take him out and flog him, and we will decide what to do with him in the morning!"

Moments later, I saw Hengist and another mercenary dragging Vortimer from the great house, stripped him of his tunic and tied him to a fence post. Laughing like a devil, Hengist produced a flagellum and struck the prince's back. Vortimer filled the courtyard with pitiable cries, but his persecutors were deaf to his suffering. It was more than I could bear. Drawing my weapons from my belt, I crept nearer the whipping post, prepared to fight the Saxons if necessary.

"Stay your hand," whispered a voice from behind me. I whirled about to face him, whoever he was, looking into the fierce, yet strangely kind face of a bearded man in clerical garb. I lowered my weapons.

Putting a finger to his lips, the cleric ambled across the courtyard leaning on a staff.

"Pardon me, good sir," said Germanus. "You would not happen to know the way to the tavern?"

"We're busy!" grumbled Hengist.

"Not too busy to do a small favor," said Germanus. "It is but a trifling thing."

"Vortigern told you to leave, old man!" said the other Saxon.

"But I have no place to lay my head. Surely there must be a tavern nearby where I might spend the cold night. Perhaps he could tell me."

The cleric pointed to a spot behind the two Saxons, prompting them to turn their heads to look. Taking this opportunity, Germanus struck Hengist in the head with the butt of his staff, rendering him unconscious. At the sound of his commander falling, the other Saxon spun about, drawing his blade to slay the cleric. I sprang from my hiding place to aid him, but Germanus had no intention of dying that night.

Drawing his own sword from beneath his cloak, Germanus countered the Saxon blade, fighting him with the skill and daring of a hardened warrior. Blood spurted from the Saxon's neck as the bishop struck a fatal blow. As the barbarian fell lifeless to the ground, Germanus cut Vortimer loose from the post, before wiping and sheathing the blade.

"Come then, lad," said Germanus. "Let us depart this wretched place. May God have mercy on their souls."

Together, we shouldered the prince and bore him out of the courtyard.

"Hefin?" said Vortimer, weakly.

"Yes, it is I."

"Good to know you, young squire," said Germanus to me. "I know of a place where we might hide for the night."

"Nay, Reverend Father," I said. "I must return to my lord Emrys' side to give a report of the city."

"Ah, a friend of Prince Emrys," said the bishop. "Good! Good!"

A Saxon curse exploded from the courtyard behind them.

"Time we should be running," said Germanus. Moving as quickly as we could, the bishop led us down a side street. The baying of hounds could be heard near at hand as we came to a small tavern. Throwing the door wide open, Germanus stepped into the tavern, bearing the burden of Vortimer.

"Germanus!" exclaimed the tavern keeper, a middle-aged man with a wolf-grey beard and balding pate. He had the look of a man who has seen much evil in this world. He immediately leapt up to relieve the bishop of his burden, helping Vortimer onto a stool.

"Bolt the door! Put out the lights!" ordered the bishop. The tavern keeper did as he was told, casting us all into darkness as the searchers passed by. Once the mercenaries had gone their way, the tavern keeper stoked up the fire again.

A woman emerged from the interior of the tavern, her eyes staring straight ahead as she groped her way along the furnishings.

"Reverend Father," she said, "what has happened?"

"Everything is alright, Rebecca," said the tavern keeper.

"I will decide whether it is alright, Andras," replied the woman.

"Vortimer here played the man and stood up to his father," replied the bishop. "Now, let us see to those wounds."

"Had you flogged, did he?" the woman named Rebecca asked.

"Aye," replied Vortimer.

"Typical."

While I am not the most skilled among my people at the healing arts, I am acquainted with the craft enough to aid those who may need it. Taking a small vial from my purse, I gently rubbed the contents on the tortured prince's back. Vortimer winced, but tried not to make a sound.

"Good lad," said Germanus. "Some elf salve will do the prince a world of good. I do not believe we have been properly introduced; I am Germanus, Bishop of Auxerre."

"A pleasure to know you, Reverend Father."

"The pleasure is mine, young sir."

"'Sir'?" inquired Rebecca. "That is not a man's voice I hear, but a maid's."

"A misunderstanding, surely," said Vortimer.

"I am blind, not deaf," replied the woman.

"She speaks truth, Vortimer," I stated. "I have been masquerading as a man for many months. I am Nimue of Avalon."

"Marvels never cease," said Vortimer. "You have fooled the world, it seems."

"But not me," said Rebecca. "I will get you some stew to bring your strength up."

"Nay, sit down, wife, I shall see to that," said Andras the tavern keeper.

"Andras, this young man has been flogged and you expect me to do nothing?"

"Alright," relented Andras. "Be careful, the cauldron is hot."

"And ice is cold and the river is wet. I know, Andras."

"My wife is very… independent," said Andras, turning to us. "Despite having lost her sight, she insists on working as hard as she did before."

"You found yourself quite a good catch, Andras," said Germanus.

"Indeed. I sometimes wonder if I deserve her."

"What do any of us really deserve, Andras?" said Rebecca, carefully setting bowls of hot stew on the table next to them. The tavern keeper put his arm about his wife's slender waist and held her close as she ran her fingers through his thinning hair.

"Now," said Germanus, "what has become of Emrys? Is he well?"

"He and a war band from Dyfed are ready to invade the city," I replied.

"Glory be to the Father and to the Son and to the Holy Ghost!" exclaimed the bishop.

"Our prayers have been answered," said Rebecca. "The king has returned!"

"He is awaiting my report on the city's defenses," I continued. "I must get word back to him quickly."

"The whole city is in an uproar," said Andras. "You should wait until morning."

"I dare them to try and catch me," I replied with a defiant smile.

There was then a loud pounding on the door.

"Open this bloody door, Andras!" barked a voice from without.

"Coming!" called Andras. In a voice barely above a whisper, he said to his guests: "It is the Saxons. You must hide!"

Leading us back to the larder, the tavern keeper indicated a spot behind some barrels of beer. I, Germanus, and Vortimer then hid in the place shown.

"Where in Wodan's name is that bishop?" growled the voice of Hengist from the common room.

"Bishop Germanus goes where the Lord leads him," said Rebecca. "How am I to know where that is?"

"He's killed one of my men," continued Hengist. "I know you've been putting him up here, and I demand to know where he is! Or maybe you need another lesson in respect."

"Is it not enough that you have taken her sight from her?" pleaded Andras. "I tell you, I know not."

"Then why are there three bowls of stew instead of two?"

"We have other guests, you know," said Rebecca. "You are welcome to search our rooms if you do not believe us."

"Very well," growled Hengist. "But if I find him..."

From within the larder, I could hear the sounds of Hengist and his men rifling through all the rooms. Eventually, the noise stopped. Hengist growled something in Saxon, slamming the door on his way out of the tavern. After a long silent pause, the larder door opened.

"It is safe to come out," said Rebecca.

"I thank you for your hospitality," I said. "But I must bring word back to Emrys."

"Of course!" said Andras. "We will ensure Vortimer is well cared for in your absence."

"Do not use the door," said Rebecca. "I will show you another way."

Rebecca led me to one of the guest rooms and threw open the shutters on the window.

"Godspeed, Nimue," said Rebecca as I climbed up on the windowsill.

"May the Almighty reward you," I replied before retreating into the darkness.

13

The queen paused in her recounting of the tale, looking to her husband.

"Well, what happened next?" asked Morgana.

"I believe that I shall allow my husband to explain the rest," said the queen.

"If you insist, good wife."

The king drew in his breath and began to tell the remainder of the story of how he defeated the legions of Vortigern and retook the kingdom.

***

A blanket of silence surrounded Londinium's southward wall as the grey-blue light of dawn rose from the eastern horizon. Gorlois and I squeezed through the narrow crevice Nimue had found.

"Now," I said, turning to Nimue, "back the way you came."

"But, my lord--!"

"Battle is not a place for a lady," I stated.

"Well, it was a few nights ago when we faced the trolls!" retorted Nimue.

I worked my jaw and said, "That was different."

"How?"

"Nimue, I thank you for bringing us this far, but for your own safety and ours, you need to be outside the walls."

"I refuse to leave your side," responded Nimue, crossing her arms.

"That's an order!"

"I am not a soldier."

"With all due respect," said Gorlois, "time is short. Settle it now, before someone hears you!"

I heaved a deep sigh. Nimue was without a doubt one of the most frustrating women I had ever met.

"Fine, but you will stay behind me at all times."

"Very well."

Up to the top of the wall we climbed, where two guardsmen stood watch over the south gate. Like a cat stalking its prey, Gorlois crept behind one of the guardsmen and slit his throat. Arrested by the sudden choking noise from his now deceased companion, the remaining guard turned his attention to us, his pale face full of shock. He did not have long to consider his predicament, however, as he found his companion's spear embedded in his chest, thrust by the hand of Gorlois.

Meanwhile, Nimue and I drew back the bolt holding the South Gate closed. The heavy doors swung open as King Kynyr blew a single blast on a brass horn, announcing the beginning of the battle. The spearmen of Britain flooded in with a mighty shout. More soldiers and mercenaries ran towards the south gate in an attempt to stop us, but it was too late.

"Kynyr," I called, "do as we planned."

Nodding his head in the affirmative, the king of Dyfed led the spearmen westward, deeper into the city, while I took command of the swordsmen.

Londinium descended into chaos. Shields and swords rang together. Nimue shot her magical bolts of fire into the opposing forces. Warriors cried out. Peasant women wailed with anguish. There was blood everywhere.

"Let God arise and let His enemies be scattered!" chanted a booming voice I had heard many times at Sunday Mass. "Let those who hate Him flee before Him!"

Cutting through the Saxon lines came a man in priestly garb, fighting like a master of sword-craft. My heart swelled with joy as I looked upon that familiar face.

"Bishop Germanus!" I shouted over the battle.

"Keep your wits about you, lad!" replied the bishop. "Now is not the time for pleasantries!"

Germanus was right, of course. I would ask about the wellbeing of my family after we had put an end to Vortigern.

My arms grew heavy from swinging the sword Caledbur. The Saxon mercenaries kept on in an endless stream of men driven mad with bloodlust, cutting, stabbing, shouting, dying. It seemed some demonic rage drove them on to greater and greater cruelty. I began to wonder if the battle was lost before it was even waged. Suddenly an agonized cry rent the air behind me. I spun around, just in time to catch Nimue before she collapsed onto the cobblestones, clutching her lower leg. A Saxon spear had flown past her, cutting her leg on the way by.

"I will be alright," she groaned.

"I will get you to safety."

A roar of laughter drew my attention. I looked up just in time to block a Saxon axe on the downswing. There stood Hengist, a cruel grin on his freckled face. I ducked as the barbarian moved in with a sweeping blow. His broad Saxon shield thwarted my attempts to strike back. Hengist, like all his folk, was a skilled warrior, knowledgeable in many weapons; keeping up with him was a challenge, but I would not allow him to harm one hair on Nimue's head.

I panted like a dog in the summer's heat as our weapons clashed. The Saxon hooked my blade in his battle axe, binding our weapons together. My head rang like a bell as Hengist struck me with his shield. I staggered backward as pain radiated through my skull. The barbarian bled from a thousand wounds.

Suddenly, he let out an agonized scream. He fell to one knee, clutching his thigh. There lay Nimue, her weapon trained on Hengist. With a mighty thrust, I impaled the Saxon through his torso. Hengist stared at the blade that had slain him, laughing mirthlessly.

"I suppose this is it, then," he said. "A short life, but we had some adventures, didn't we, lad?"

I pulled Caledbur from the dying Saxon, saying not a word.

"I don't take it personally," continued Hengist as he bled. "You're a mighty warrior. You'll make a fine king."

With that, the barbarian expired. The noise of battle continued on around me, but time seemed frozen in that moment. I once thought the Saxons little better than beasts, but perhaps there was nobility in them after all.

"Thank you," I said to Nimue.

"You are welcome, good prince."

Bending down, I raised Nimue up and carried her down a side street.

"Leave me here," she said. "I will only slow you down."

"You refused to leave my side; I shall not leave yours either," I stated in reply.

"But the men," she pleaded, "they need someone to lead them."

I ground my teeth; she was right, after all. I could not quit the battle for one wounded warrior, even if that warrior was a dear friend. These are the hard choices a good king must make.

As I weighed this in my mind, the booming voice of Bishop Germanus erupted somewhere behind me. I whirled around as the holy man strode toward me, his white robes stained with blood.

"Ah, Nimue," he said, observing my burden. "Wounded yourself, did you? Well, that will teach you. Battle is no place for a lady."

"It could have happened to any man," groaned Nimue.

"Give her here, lad, I will make certain she is cared for."

"But--" I protested, but the Bishop insisted.

Leaving Nimue in good hands, I emerged from the side street into one of the main roads, my sword in my hand.

"Come men!" I cried. "To the great house!"

With a mighty cheer, the warriors of Dyfed charged toward the house of the usurper, fighting through what remained of the Saxon mercenaries and whatever inhuman monsters Ceridwen had conjured for us.

Enormous black dogs charged through the street; they were the unholy creation of Tegid and Ceridwen: hounds in shape, but possessing a rational soul. A dog only does as it is told by training and instinct; these beasts were evil by nature, filled with malice.

Foam dripped from their jaws as they charged in for the attack. One of them lunged toward me, snarling. With an upward stroke from Caledbur, I severed his foul head from his body.. Another came around behind, taking my cloak in his teeth and dragging me to the ground. It would have put an end to me, but I rolled out of the way in time, and ran it through with the mighty sword.

Undaunted by my encounters with the animals, I pressed forward, arriving at the great house as the sun reached the center of the sky.

"Come out, coward!" I called as I thrust open the door. "Come and face me like a man!"

But there was no answer to my taunts. I searched the entire house, frightening the servants, but I found no trace of Vortigern.

"My lord," said Gorlois. "I have searched all the house and grounds; Vortigern is gone."

I uttered a curse. "That craven poltroon!"

Venting my rage, I chopped an ornate chair in half with a single blow from Caledbur. Kicking the pieces away, I strode out to the courtyard, roaring with rage at having been cheated out of my vengeance. A motley crowd had gathered about the house; among them were those I had come to call my friends.

"Vortimer!" I called delightedly, spying him in the throng.

The prince moved to the fore of the crowd, joined by a peasant couple.

"You are truly a sight for sore eyes, good prince," said Vortimer.

"I heard you received quite the flogging on my account," I replied.

"Indeed, but I consider it but a trifling thing. After many years of cowering before my father, it was good to feel brave."

Taking a step backward, the prince gestured to the peasants by his sides.

"These have cared for my wounds. Andras and his wife, Rebecca. They have ever remained loyal to the memory of Custennin, even to their own pain."

The peasants bowed respectfully before me. "Your Majesty," said they.

"Thank you for caring for my friend," I said. "Your kindness shall not go unrewarded."

"We ask no reward," said Andras, "but only that you put an end to Vortigern."

"Oh, I have every intention of doing so."

"Hail Emrys!" shouted Kynyr the Red, made redder by the blood of foemen. "Is the day won?"

"The day is ours, King Kynyr!" I called.

Kynyr and his spearmen threw back their heads and raised a a loud shout of triumph, waving their weapons in the air.

"Told ye we could do it!" he said, engulfing me in a joyful embrace. "Custennin is avenged!"

"Nay, Kynyr," I corrected. "Not yet. The usurper has fled the city."

"Chicken-hearted dastard!" spat Kynyr.

Pushing aside the gathering throng came Bishop Germanus, a wide grin on his saintly face. By his side limped Nimue, her leg bandaged and appearing otherwise quite whole.

"Reverend Father! Lady Nimue!" I cried joyfully.

"Good to see you again, lad!" exclaimed Germanus. "You have made quite an accounting for yourself for one so young. Your skill with the blade is improving."

"It pleases me to hear you say that, Father," I replied. I turned my attention to the lady warrior and said: "Are you well, Nimue?"

"I will be alright in time," replied the princess with a smile. "I am already healing."

I grinned. "These are good tidings indeed. Reverend Father, have you tidings of my mother and brother?"

"They are quite well, though worried to the point of madness for you."

"I shall send for them once I have put an end to Vortigern."

"Why have you not put an end to him already?" asked Nimue.

"It seems he has departed the city."

"Aye, flown the coop like the fowl he is!" shouted Kynyr.

"We shall catch him yet," I said.

"In the meantime, I'm famished!" said Kynyr. "Where can a man get some food around these parts?"

I too was quite hungered and exhausted from my efforts and a hearty meal and a long sleep would not have gone amiss.

We therefore paraded into the mead hall and sat down at the great oaken board therein. The servants provided us with whatever food we asked for; they seemed almost relieved that the master of the house had gone. Singing songs of victory, we toasted our victory with the usurper's finest wine and mead. Indeed, it was a gladsome time for all, though admittedly, I remember very little of it. What with the wine and mead and the fatigue from battle, my memory of that evening is dulled. I will not forget, however, the joy and triumph of that day, nor the mighty deeds done thereupon.

14

It was early in the morning when I arose from sleep in the luxurious bedchamber of Vortigern. I did not recall having gone to bed; I presumed that the servants had taken me there after a night of feasting. Stretching my sore arms over my head, I set about preparing for whatever the day had in store.

Entering the mead hall, I found Germanus, Kynyr, Gorlois, Vortimer, and Nimue awaiting me.

"Your highness!" cried Kynyr. "We thought you would never awaken!"

I greeted all of those gathered in the hall, taking my seat across the table from Nimue, who seemed none the worse for the wear after the previous day's excitement.

"How are you faring today, my lady?" I inquired.

"I am in good health," replied lady Nimue.

"It pleases me that you are well," I said.

"As it pleases me that you are well, good prince," replied Nimue.

I smiled; while I knew her to be a formidable warrior, I had begun to see her as quite a lovely woman.

"Where do you suppose your father has gone, Vortimer?" I inquired.

"Back to his tower in the mountain country, such as it is," replied Vortimer.

"Then we'll chase that fox to ground!" said Kynyr.

"Hear hear!" said Vortimer.

"Nay, Vortimer," I retorted. "You are still healing from your lashes. Furthermore, I need someone to care for Londinium, and I can think of no one better."

Vortimer nodded gravely.

"You bestow upon me a great honor, King Emrys."

It was the first time anyone had addressed me as "King". I felt as if the world was finally being put right again after many years of being wrong; almost like the first breath of spring after a long, cold winter.

"No, not a king yet," said Germanus. "But we can remedy that."

Germanus rose from his seat and directed all to do the same. Turning to the company, he said: "Sirs, I here present unto you Emrys, son of

Custennin, your undoubted King. Wherefore all you who are come this day to do your homage and service, are you willing to do the same?"

"We are," came the reply.

Turning back to me, the bishop administered the oath of sovereignty.

"Will you solemnly promise and swear to govern the Peoples of the Kingdom of Logres according to their respective laws and customs?"

"I solemnly promise to do so," I replied.

"Will you to your power cause Law and Justice, in Mercy, to be executed in all your judgments?"

"I will."

"Will you to the utmost of your power maintain the Laws of God and the true profession of the Gospel?"

"All this I promise to do. The things which I have here before promised, I will perform, and keep, so help me God."

Entering the mead hall came Andras bearing a codex of the Holy Scripture.

"Here is Wisdom," said Germanus. "This is the royal Law; These are the lively Oracles of God."

We then celebrated the Eucharist together in that hall. Vortigern had torn down all the churches or profaned them with his devilry. However, Our Lord used a common table in an upper room as His altar, and Germanus saw it fit to do the same.

After hymns and prayers, the Bishop led me to a great oaken chair and directed me to sit. Opening a bottle of holy oil, Germanus anointed my head and my hands, praying as he did so. He then placed a golden ring upon my finger; Custennin's signet ring.

Vortimer approached my throne, bearing a wreath of holly. The bishop took the holly wreath and, blessing it, placed the wreath upon my head.

In a loud voice, all in attendance cried out: "God save the king!"

Continuing with the rite, Germanus prayed: "God crown you with a crown of glory and righteousness, that having a right faith and manifold fruit of good works, you may obtain the crown of an everlasting kingdom by the gift of him whose kingdom endureth for ever."

"Amen!" said all emphatically.

Closing with another hymn, Germanus said many blessings over me, after which we all arose and processed to the courtyard.

"Behold your king!" proclaimed Bishop Germanus, spreading his hands wide.

Drawing the sword Caledbur, I held it high saluting the men of Dyfed and all others who had gathered without. The citizenry of Londinium stood about us, seeming confused or lost. One could hardly blame them; their accustomed king had forsaken them, after all.

"People of Londinium," I said in a loud voice. "My fellow Britons, I am Emrys, heir of King Custennin; the true king. Vortigern's false kingship is at an end. He shall soon be vanquished. His son, Vortimer, shall rule Londinium as my proconsul. You will listen to him and do everything he says."

"Thank you, my lord," said Vortimer.

"Thank *you*, Vortimer."

Placing the sword back into the scabbard, I looked about me at the faces of my fellows. Excitement and anticipation written on every countenance; they were ready to follow me on our next adventure.

"We shall depart for the mountains as soon as we can do so," I stated.

Kynyr let out a hearty laugh and ordered his men to make ready for departure.

Once we had eaten and done on our battle gear, the men and I gathered in the street, ready to set out. I had nearly mounted my horse when Nimue drew near, a sorrowful expression on her slender face.

"Would that you could accompany us," I remarked. "You showed more courage and honor than many a trained warrior."

"Such was not meant for me," she sighed. "I would only hinder your progress."

"Do not weep," I said, gently wiping away her tears. "I shall return, once the usurper is dead."

"Do you promise?"

I tenderly touched my lips to her forehead.

"I promise."

Placing my helmet atop my head, I got onto my horse and gave the order to leave.

"Godspeed, King Emrys!" cried Nimue over the clatter of our horses' hooves.

Out we rode from the Londinium toward the northwest, back toward that cursed mountain country which I thought I would never return to. The hand of vengeance was heavy upon me, driving me to put an end to the usurper's reign of corruption. I had no thought in my mind but destruction.

15

Into the wilds we rode, following the track of Vortigern back to that cold mountain country that I had come to hate. Onward we went as the sun sank into the western sea. I gave the order to halt, which Kynyr relayed to the men with his loud brass horn.

"We will stay here for the night," I said as we entered a forested glen. "Let us make camp."

The men did as they were told, pitching their tents and making campfires to stave off the cold and gloom. I meanwhile slipped away into the wood. We were drawing near to the cursed city of Bala; I could feel its shadow all about me. I knew that Lord Tegid and his devils would do everything in their power to prevent me from accomplishing my goal of destroying Vortigern. I therefore sought the council of the Almighty, dropping to my knees beyond the edge of camp.

The light of the half-moon poured down through the bare tree branches and onto the forest floor like water pouring from a pitcher. As I made my petitions, however, a thick cloud rolled in, obscuring the moon's silver face. A cold breeze whistled through the boughs. The hair stood up on the back of my neck; I was not alone.

I arose from my knees, drawing Caledbur, ready to fight whatever it was that was hunting me.

"Who goes there?" I spoke into the darkness. Then came a whispering voice, as though the wind spoke. "I am the Night. I am Death."

My heart quickened as beads of cold sweat formed on my forehead. Out of the corner of my eye, I saw a black shape standing a few feet away, but as I turned to face it, it vanished like smoke.

"Who are you?" asked the voice.

"I am King Emrys," I responded.

"King? By what right do you call yourself king?"

The shape materialized again. Whirling about, I lashed out with my sword, only to watch it disappear again.

"I am the son of Custennin!"

"You lie," hissed the voice. "You are no son of Custennin. You are a usurper, just like Vortigern."

"No!" I cried as I slashed the darkness with my sword once again.

"If they knew what you were..." whispered the voice again.

Torchlight illuminated the darkness. Loud and clear came the voice of Bishop Germanus, who had insisted on accompanying us to the tower.

"Begone, she-devil!" he commanded. "Return to Bala! Tell your lover we are coming!"

Out of the gloom came what I can only assume was a curse in the damnable tongue of Annwyn, followed by a cold rush of wind.

I sheathed my blade with a shudder; I had come face to face with Ceridwen herself, the mistress of evil.

"Are you alright, my son?" asked the bishop.

"I will be," I replied.

"What did she say to you?"

I hesitated. What would happen if I told Bishop Germanus all that she and Vortimer had told me?

"She told me that I am not truly the son of Custennin. That I am a usurper, like Vortigern."

Germanus paused, a pained expression on his face.

"It is a partial truth," he said. My heart sank. "Custennin is not truly your father."

"Then who is?"

"No one knows for certain. Someone --or something-- masquerading as Custennin seduced your mother. She could hardly be blamed for it. Custennin, being a gracious man, raised you as his own son."

Anger swelled within my breast.

"Then why did you make me king if you knew I was not legitimate?"

"Because it was Custennin's will that it be so," replied the bishop. "As far as he or anyone else is concerned, you are the true king."

I sighed deeply. At last I knew the truth, though it only filled me with more questions. It gratified me to know that Custennin had loved my mother enough to hide the matter, and furthermore that he trusted me enough to leave the kingdom in my hands, despite my questionable origins. Still, I wondered who my father could possibly be. Obviously a great magician of some kind or another had fathered me, which might explain my visions of future events.

Weariness from travel and my struggle against the witch overwhelmed me and I went immediately to my tent, where I collapsed into a deep slumber.

16

Another grey morning drifted over those wretched hills as we broke camp and continued on the road to the tower. A silent foreboding hung over us like a cold mist of dread as the snow fell down upon us. All of a sudden there was about us the sound of hoofbeats of hundreds of horses. We halted, drawing our weapons in preparation for the foe.

"Stand your ground!" I cried.

Over a ridge of hills they came, but these were no soldiers of Bala, nor were they Saxon. Clothed in gleaming armor and riding fantastic steeds, they rode into the little valley toward us. At their head road one of kingly bearing, wearing an exquisitely inlaid war-mask and carrying a mighty spear.

"Emrys, son of Custennin," said the war-leader, "be not alarmed; we are friends of Britain."

"Prince Gwyn!" cried Germanus.

"Germanus?" said the war leader, cocking his head to one side.

"It has been what? Two and twenty years? Good to see you again!"

I sheathed my sword, realizing that this was none other than the war band of Avalon.

"Indeed, it is good to see you again, good father," said Prince Gwyn. "Still fighting, I see."

"You could not keep me away from this battle!"

Many in the church were not in favor of the bishop's habit of charging into battle, but none of them could stop him, either.

Turning to me, the elf tilted his head and said, "My sister informs me that you are in need of our help. We would be honored to fight by your side, King Emrys."

"The honor is mine, good prince," I replied. "We will put an end to Vortigern together."

The highwaymen and the men of Dyfed raised a great shout. Over the hills we rode, until we came within sight of the tower.

However, Vortigern had prepared for our arrival. Saxon men, soldiers of Annwyn, and beasts of every shape, some of them so horrific as to be impossible to describe, rushed toward us in a furious flood of hate. Kynyr's voice rose to a lion-like roar, urging his men onward. Gwyn blew his great war-horn, and I uttered an ancient battle-cry as we faced the approaching horrors.

Swords flew from their scabbards, immediately setting about the work of hewing down man and beast. The fiery fighting spirit of the Britons burned hot in my blood as I cut and thrust my sword into the horrors. Gwyn and Kynyr hefted their spears into the foe, fighting for all their worth. Gorlois and his men loosed a deadly rain of arrows and stones. Bishop Germanus charged headlong into the adversaries, lopping off heads and limbs like a husbandman tending trees.

My horse fell dead beneath me, a Saxon spear shaft protruding from his side. It is such a pity when a horse dies in battle. War horses are brave beasts; they did not ask for war, but are merely witless beasts who do the bidding of their masters. I was sorry to lose such a good mount; he had been faithful through the mountain country.

Like ravenous carrion crows, Tegid's devils set upon me. A hound's head fell to earth as I swung Caledbur to my right. Another inhuman met his end upon my blade as I stabbed left. The creatures of Bala were upon me, licking their lips at the prospect of tasting my blood. Soon there were simply too many of them for me to fight, Caledbur or no. But this was not to be my end, as one of my adversaries suddenly discovered a long spear shaft in his guts: a gift from Prince Gwyn. With surprising speed and accuracy, many arrows found their targets in my foes, as Gorlois' bowstring sang a song of battle.

"Ha! Take that, you heathen dogs!" cried Bishop Germanus as he relieved a Saxon of his head. Having dispatched all of the adversaries in the immediate vicinity, the three gathered about me, helping me extricate myself from the dead horse.

"We all promised Nimue that we would not allow you to come to any harm," said Gorlois. "A promise we intend to keep."

"When this is over, Gorlois," said I, "I will grant you lands and a title."

"That is awfully generous, good king."

Looking up at the hill fort, I watched as Lord Tegid stood upon an unfinished turret, looking down into the tumult below. With a single motion from his gnarled hand, the mountain split open with a resounding crack. Out of the fissure came a fearsome sight; two Conqueror Wyrms, one red, the other white, emerged, writhing from the darkness. The armies retreated in terror before the fearsome sight; only myself and my three companions remained.

The bishop blessed me with the sign of the Cross, saying: "Thou shalt tread upon the lion and adder: the young lion and the dragon shalt thou trample under feet."

Through the blood-stained morass of the battlefield, Gwyn and I marched toward the serpents, ready to send them back into the primeval darkness from which they came.

The white dragon looked on me with an expression of pure hatred. Throwing off its red counterpart, the massive reptile slithered nearer me, bellowing loudly, its sulfurous breath filling my nostrils. I narrowly avoided a snap from its great jaws, swiping at its snout with Caledbur on its way by. Again, it came in for the attack, but the red wyrm bit into its tail and dragged it backward. The white dragon beat it off with a swat from its great back paw, turning its attention back to me. A horrible moan emanated from its jaws as it whirled its head about. Prince Gwyn had pierced the beast's side with his mighty spear, but this seemed only to anger it.

The white wyrm chased after its elvish prey, but the red pounced atop it, holding it down by the neck like a lion killing a deer. I saw my opportunity; howling like a wolf of war, I charged in, blade aimed at the serpent. The white wyrm let out a gurgling grunt as Caledbur bit deep into its throat, black blood spewing from its wound.

Leaping backward to a safe distance, I watched as the beast writhed in the throes of death; its violent contortions could have easily crushed me. At last, the white wyrm lay still. Approaching the corpse, I laid hold of my sword, still lodged in the creature's thick skin. However, just as I seized the ancient hilt, a deep rumbling sound arrested my attention. I looked up into the face of the red dragon, its yellow eyes regarding me, not with malice nor hunger; it almost seemed as though the creature had come to thank me for my aid.

We paused, looking at one another for a moment, before the reptilian head turned away and the red serpent lumbered off into the wilds. I stood there for a moment, wondering if not all dragons were bent entirely on chaos; perhaps there are some that are benevolent. However, I had no time to reflect on this.

I looked about me to see what had become of Gwyn. I found him, healthy and whole, pulling his famous spear from the back of the dead dragon.

"Are you whole, good prince?" I asked.

"Hale and hearty!" replied the elf prince.

"Then let us put an end to this!"

Turning my eyes to the hillfort again, I watched as Tegid spread his black cloak, transformed into a massive bat, and flew away from the battle. To the tower we went, fighting our way through opposing forces, up the stone steps to the unfinished structure. Finally, we came to the tower, where a cohort of Saxons stood guard at the door. The barbarians charged toward us, swinging their swords and battle axes. I narrowly dodged several blows from a short sword, and cut deep into its owner's torso. Gwyn, meanwhile, impaled another on the point of his spear, fighting off their companions with a long knife.

"Go, Emrys!" cried Gwyn. "I will hold them off! Get to Vortigern!"

Without another word, I ran inside the castle. Finding him not on the ground floor, I ascended a flight of steps, slew two more mercenaries, and came to an upper chamber. There I found him, hiding like the rodent he was.

"Your end has come, tyrant!" I cried.

The usurper drew his blade, standing ready for a fight. I responded with a mighty swing of my sword. Vortigern dodged the attack, striking at me with his own blade. Vortigern was a formidable opponent, made even more so by my own fatigue from the battle. My limbs were heavy. My lungs burned within my chest. However, I was determined to put an end to the usurper.

All of my teachers in the arts of warfare had taught me never to fight angry. Anger makes one liable to make foolish mistakes. I hated what Vortigern had done, but I could not allow my hatred to cloud my judgment. I tried not to see him as Vortigern; to me, he was no more than a common soldier of above average skill.

Suddenly there was a great flash of light and a sound like thunder. I thought that the tower had been struck by lightning, but no. I glanced out the window to see such crafts as I had never before witnessed in my life: the majestic flying ships of Avalon sailing overhead, buffeting the tower with their flaming projectiles.

A surge of pain filled my mind; distracted by the awesome sight out the window, I had allowed the usurper an opening to cut into my right thigh. Staggering backward, I countered a nearly fatal blow, and moved in for another attack.

I suddenly became aware of an odor; the scent of burning timber permeated my nostrils. The tower was on fire. We choked on the thick smoke engulfing us in its hellish embrace. The flames were soon upon us, spreading over the timbers. I am not ashamed to say that I was not a little alarmed by the flames; life, while difficult, was sweet to me and I had no desire to forfeit it in my youth. Still, if this was to be my end, then I would accept it bravely, taking the usurper with me.

Vortigern suddenly halted his onslaught, breathless, choking on the fumes. I moved in to strike, but the usurper side-stepped just in time. Fire consumed the floorboards between us.

"Emrys!" called a voice. I spun about at the sound. Gwyn stood at the doorway, his hand outstretched toward me.

I realized then that escape from this inferno would soon be impossible. I could either leave with my life or slay Vortigern; and I chose life. Taking Gwyn's hand, I leapt over the gap in the floor, and we fled down the stairs as quickly as our feet could take us. We escaped just in time; another flaming bolt from the elvish war engines ripped through the tower. Thus the evil reign of Vortigern was ended. I expected to feel something; I had finally avenged my father, after all. I should have felt some sort of relief, but I felt rather hollow. Justice had been done, but it did not bring Custennin back. I took consolation in that I was king now, and had no rivals to contend with.

As I limped down the hillside to the valley below, Gwyn supported me with his shoulder.

"Thank you, good prince," I said.

"You are most welcome," said Gwyn. "I am more than happy to support the high king of Britain."

"Hail King Emrys!" shouted Germanus. "Custennin is avenged!"

A loud cheer went up from the men as we reached the bottom of the hill. King Kynyr descended from his horse, clapping me hard on the back. I grunted; the last few days had been hard on my body and I was feeling the strain of combat.

Raising me up on their shoulders, the two men bore me away from the tower amidst the victorious songs of our valiant troops.

17

The stonemasons worked busily on the hilltop, cutting, measuring, leveling, and shoring up the ruined tower. I paced about the fortress observing the men in their labors, my mother, Adhan, holding my arm.

"It is a fine tower indeed," said my mother. "Will this be your capitol?"

"Nay, mother," I replied. "Too close to Bala. This shall be a warbase."

"And what of Londinium?"

"I gave Londinium to Vortimer, and I shall not take it back now; he is doing good work there, rebuilding the old churches and some new ones. The peasants have even started calling him 'Saint Vortimer'. We will use Father's old capital, Camelot."

"I heard there was a new treaty drawn up," my mother said abruptly.

"Aye," I affirmed. "Lord Arawn has agreed to withdraw all influence from the world of men, save for Bala. Unfortunately, so has King Nudd."

"We are on our own, then."

"So it would seem. Perhaps it is for the best that we stand on our own feet."

"Perhaps."

We quietly admired the tower that I would eventually name Dynas Emrys; I was king, after all, I had earned the right to make a name for myself.

I turned to look at my mother. "Custennin was not my father, was he?" I asked, more as a statement than a question.

She went silent, looking away from me as a tear slid down her cheek.

"How did you find out?"

"Bishop Germanus explained what happened. I just had to hear it from your lips."

"It is true."

I stood in silence, searching for words.

"What will we tell Uther?" I asked.

"Nothing for now. When he's a bit older, perhaps."

I nodded gravely. The sound of a slight cough interrupted our conversation. Nimue stood a short distance away, clothed in a yellow gown embroidered with leaves and flowers, a green cloak hanging from her shoulders. Her lustrous dark hair was returning after she had shorn it to create the illusion of masculinity.

"My lady," I said enthusiastically. "It pleases me to see you again."

"It is good to see you as well, noble king," replied the elf princess with a smile.

"I would like to introduce you to my mother, Adhan."

"A pleasure to meet you, fair queen of Britain," said Nimue with a slight bow.

"The pleasure is mine, Lady Nimue," replied my mother. "I understand you were of great help to my son on this adventure; he has hardly stopped talking about your acts of bravery."

Nimue gave a slight chuckle.

"I never properly thanked you for your aid in the fight," I said to the elf. "You were a fine warrior."

"As are you."

"If you will excuse me, Lady Nimue," said Mother, "there is a matter I must attend to."

My mother wandered off somewhere, leaving the two of us alone on the hillside.

"I think I like you better as a maid," I stated.

"I prefer being one, although I did enjoy some parts of being a man for a time," she replied. "Armor, fighting, not being told what to do."

I laughed.

"Even kings must take orders sometimes."

"What is the point of being king then?" said Nimue with a wry smile.

"You get the largest house, servants, armies, horses, and all the free mead you can drink."

We both laughed, but there was a bitterness to our laughter.

"I suppose we will not be seeing much of one another," I said, grimly.

"I suppose not," she replied. "For a time, but not forever. Perhaps one day, I will be permitted to return to this fair isle."

I nodded, smiling slightly.

"You will have an honored place in my court when that day should come."

Nimue blushed.

"Until then," she said, taking a step forward. The beautiful elf-maiden pressed her soft red lips into mine for a moment that seemed far too short.

"Farewell, King Emrys."

She turned away from me and walked off into the wilderness. I sighed longingly, watching her until she vanished into the foliage. The sound of Uther shouting my name interrupted my reverie.

"Come then, King Laggard! We have Saxons to kill!"

"Of course," I replied, laughing.

With that, we mounted our horses and rode away eastward toward our next battle.

Epilogue

King Emrys took a long draught of mead, having finished his tale. All in attendance agreed that it was a good tale, and well told, and we toasted the king's prowess. That is, all except for Uther. He sat silent at the table with a dour expression on his face; not an unusual experience, to be sure, but I deemed that he was disgruntled about something his brother said.

"And I assure you," said Queen Nimue, "every word of it is true."

"Hear hear!" said Kynyr, draining his horn.

The hour was late, and the guests were weary; some had already fallen asleep. The king and queen bade them goodnight, and the servants escorted them to their chambers.

"Come then, love," said Creirwy. "Come to bed."

As my wife and I walked hand in hand down the passage to our chamber, I heard the sound of Uther's voice speaking in an angry tone.

"Are you certain it was wise to reveal to half the nobles of the kingdom your dubious parentage?" he asked in a hoarse voice.

"What of it?" replied the king, calmly.

"We may lose their support!"

Emrys sighed.

"Uther, have you learned nothing? All authority is based on mutual trust, and dedication to the truth. I will not have a kingdom founded on deception. What they think about me is not our concern, nor are we to worry ourselves with it. Victory is not to be founded solely on strength of arms."

There was a long pause.

"Very well," Uther relented.

"Sometimes by admitting what is shameful," added Emrys, "we become greater than the shame of it, and we lead others to become greater as well."

"This is true, brother," said Uther.

"Goodnight, Uther," said Emrys. "Sleep well, and be not anxious about the opinions of others."

"Gwion!" hissed Creirwy. She was leaning upon the doorpost of our chamber, looking rather annoyed. "Enough eavesdropping. Come to bed!"

I smiled and followed my wife into our chamber for a long winter's sleep.

Made in the USA
Monee, IL
17 February 2022

91384419R00059